Rowan Hood
Returns

THE TALES OF ROWAN HOOD
By Nancy Springer

ROWAN HOOD, OUTLAW GIRL OF SHERWOOD FOREST

LIONCLAW

OUTLAW PRINCESS OF SHERWOOD

WILD BOY

Rowan Hood Returns

The Final Chapter

Nancy Springer

Philomel Books ❦ New York

PHILOMEL BOOKS
A division of Penguin Young Readers Group
Published by The Penguin Group
Penguin Group (USA) Inc., 375 Hudson Street, New York, NY 10014, U.S.A.
Penguin Group (Canada), 10 Alcorn Avenue, Toronto, Ontario, Canada M4V 3B2
(a division of Pearson Penguin Canada Inc.)
Penguin Books Ltd, 80 Strand, London WC2R 0RL, England.
Penguin Ireland, 25 St. Stephen's Green, Dublin 2, Ireland (a division of Penguin Books Ltd.)
Penguin Books India Pvt Ltd, 11 Community Centre, Panchsheel Park, New Delhi - 110 017, India.
Penguin Group (NZ), Cnr Airborne and Rosedale Roads, Albany, Auckland, New Zealand
(a division of Pearson New Zealand Ltd.)
Penguin Books (South Africa) (Pty) Ltd, 24 Sturdee Avenue, Rosebank, Johannesburg 2196, South Africa.
Penguin Books Ltd, Registered Offices: 80 Strand, London WC2R 0RL, England.

Printed in the United States of America.
Design by Gunta Alexander. Text set in Apollo.

Library of Congress Cataloging-in-Publication Data
Springer, Nancy. Rowan Hood returns : the final chapter / Nancy Springer.
p. cm.   Sequel to: Wild boy, a tale of Rowan Hood.
Summary: When she finds out who murdered her mother, Celandine,
Rowan Hood returns to her former home to seek revenge.
[1. Revenge—Fiction. 2. Adventure and adventurers—Fiction. 3. Elves—Fiction. 4. Robin Hood
(Legendary character)—Fiction. 5. Great Britain—History—Richard I, 1189–1199—Fiction.] I. Title.
PZ7.S76846Rr 2005   [Fic]—dc22   2004020319

ISBN 0-399-24206-6
1 3 5 7 9 10 8 6 4 2
First Impression

To Jaime

One

On a stony slope above the Nottingham Way, Rowan gathered coltsfoot with her dagger, harvesting the hardy flower roots and all. Nearby, her bow lay at the ready, strung, with short flint-tipped arrows close at hand. Her wolf-dog, Tykell, lay nearby also, basking in the first warm sunshine of spring.

But not at ease. With his head lifted, he tested the messages in the air as Rowan worked. And she also kept watch. As she dropped each plant, yellow sunburst blossom and hoof-shaped leaves and root, into her sack, she scanned the heathery wasteland, careful never to stray too far from the edge of Sherwood Forest. The sheriff's men had caught her out here in the open once, but they would not catch her again—

"Tag. You're It," said a man's soft voice close to her ear, directly behind her.

Rowan barely kept from screaming out loud as she leapt up and away, turning in midair, landing in a fighter's crouch to face—

A tall man in stagskin boots, brown woolen leggings and a green jerkin. A handsome, grinning man with blond curls out of control beneath his cap, his sky-blue eyes twinkling bright with fun.

"Father," Rowan gasped, straightening, panting to regain the breath he had startled out of her. "Toads take it, you scared me inside out."

Tykell, who knew Robin Hood well, yawned and wagged his tail.

"Shame on you," Rowan told the wolf-dog, "in cahoots with this scoundrel." To her father she complained, "*Must* you practice your stalking on me?"

Chuckling, Robin Hood hugged his daughter and kissed her on the side of her head, on her smooth brown hair drawn back into a braid. "Just keeping you sharp and wary," he told her. "*Must* you venture out here?"

"It's where the coltsfoot grows." The open, stony upland ran along the forest like a yellow river, furze and coltsfoot both in bloom, while the budding oaks of Sherwood Forest towered above, kingly trees crowned with mistletoe. Rowan turned her head to scan the Nottingham Way, which curved outside the forest at this point, downslope from where she stood. Seeing no one there, she breathed out.

"Well, it's not much safer in the forest," Robin admitted, standing back from her and scanning for danger in his turn. "I came looking for you, lass, to tell you that the merry men and I will be on the move for a while."

Rowan nodded, knowing this was the most dangerous time of the year for Robin and his comrades. With the warmer weather of early spring, the ground had softened to provide good tracking for outlaw hunters, but the trees were not yet in leaf to provide concealment for the outlaws. The king's foresters and other bounty hunters were swarming Sherwood Forest in pursuit of human prey.

But last year Robin hadn't gone on the run. Rowan asked, "Is it worse than usual this spring?"

"Yes, because the winter was harsh." Beyond being the most dangerous time of year, this was also the hungriest season—for all common folk, not just for outlaws. Peasants gathered lamb's lettuce and other greens at the edge of the forest, but it was no use trying to trade them meat for bread or cheese; they had none. They had used up all their stores of grain over the winter. Their starving cows had not yet freshened to give milk. Sometimes desperate peasants ventured into the forest, trying to hunt game for meat. And they were clumsy about it, getting themselves caught by the foresters and frightening the deer, making the outlaws' lot even harder.

"We still have stores of dried fish," Rowan offered, "and walnuts and such."

"You're marvels, you youngsters. But keep your fish. And keep yourselves safe." Robin hugged Rowan again, this time in farewell, then held her at arm's length by the shoulders to look at her. "Will you be all right?"

"Yes. Of course."

"You'll be able to find me if you need me?"

The *aelfin* blood in Rowan gave her certain powers: to comfort and heal with the touch of a hand, to sense the presence of hidden sweetwater, and lately, to similarly sense where in Sherwood was Robin Hood.

"Of course," Rowan repeated. "Be more mindful of yourself, Father, to come to no harm."

"I will, with the blessing of the Lady. Until we meet again, then." Robin Hood bent to kiss her once more, this time on the forehead. Then, turning quickly, he strode into the forest.

Rowan blinked, sighed, looked all around her for any sign of danger, then bent to her task again, gathering coltsfoot.

The first flower of spring, coltsfoot. A goodly plant, the dried blossom good for tinder to start a cooking fire, the whole green plant or the dried leaves good for boiling into a tea that would clear the head of phlegm.

Rowan's eyes did not clear. They filled with tears.

Remembering: a day in early springtime when she had gathered coltsfoot, then returned home only to scatter the golden blossoms on her mother's burned, dead body.

"Toads take it, what's the matter with me?" Rowan grumbled at herself in a whisper. "That was two years ago."

It didn't matter. Even the sunny air felt dark with the memory of that day. And now with new grief, her father's going away—though of course she had put a brave face to that. In a sense, Rowan realized, she had lied to Robin. In truth, she did not feel as if she was going to be all right "of course." All day she had been feeling an inner darkening, a chill in her bones, an inkling of—what? Some new peril?

Not peril exactly, but . . . foreboding.

Wiping her eyes on her sleeve, Rowan straightened to look around again, at the hazel, elder and blackthorn bushes edging Sherwood Forest, then the uplands, prickly with furze, then the stony meandering of the Nottingham Way—she saw no one on that road, not even a tinker in his donkey cart or a black-robed Wanderer plodding, though she traced its course almost to the horizon. There in the distance, soft hills billowed the color of a rock dove. Rowan heard jays confabulating in the oaks, saw plovers flying in the blue sky—the day could not have seemed more peaceful. Yet within herself she felt a storm building, and she didn't know why.

That morning, as she had left her rowan grove, the slender trees had whispered and sighed to her: *Good-bye, good-bye.* As if she might never return. As if she might die.

Something was going to happen.

Rowan felt a trembling urge to flee into the forest, hide somewhere, or better yet, find Father and go with him. . . . But she shook her head at herself and bent once more to gather coltsfoot. "No use running from it, whatever it is," she remarked to Tykell.

Panting a white-fanged grin at her, the wolf-dog waved his plumy tail amid dried stems of last year's thistles, rattling their sere heads.

Behind the rustling of the thistles, Rowan heard another sound, a kind of tapping or clattering. Something with hooves moving on stones. Tykell lay calmly panting, so it could not be anything dangerous. Deer, perhaps, venturing out of the forest to feed on scant new grass. Two summers ago, when first she had found her way to Sherwood Forest, Rowan would have stalked the deer, shot one and shared the meat with the other members of her band. But now her injured legs would not let her hunt deer. She remained bent over her work, eyes on the stony ground, as the clattering sound grew nearer.

It wasn't deer. Something larger.

Galloping toward her!

Jerking her head up, Rowan gasped and snatched for her bow and arrows. A horseman! Or not a man, but a young squire on a white pony—bad enough. Some lord's henchman in the making. Half-helm shadowing his face, quilted tabard armoring his chest, shield riding like a full copper moon on his arm, short sword lashed to his left leg. In a moment he would draw the weapon and, if she let him near her, he would lop off her head and tie it by the hair to his saddle, then ride to Nottingham to collect his hundred pounds of gold, or whatever bounty was to be got for a dead outlaw these days.

In one quick movement Rowan nocked her arrow and leaned her weight into the horns of her bow, bending it almost double. There was nothing she, a healer, hated worse than killing, but she'd done it before, to survive. Or to help a comrade survive. On that day they'd captured her, she had killed three men so that Beau could get away. Then Nottingham's men had overpowered Rowan and roped her arms to her sides, but perforce they had let her weapon lie; the bow and short flint-tipped arrows, gifts of the *aelfe,* had burned their fingers like fire, and they could not touch them.

Now, facing the approaching rider with her bow-string drawn back so far that the feathers of her elf-bolt touched her ear, Rowan spoke no threat. She didn't have to. The bow and arrow spoke for her. And Tykell—

But what was wrong with Tykell? He had not growled a warning, and now, when he should have been bristling and snarling and roaring at the stranger, in-stead he trotted forward with his furry tail sweeping a smile in the air.

And the rider did not even draw rein. "Rowan, it's just me," he called.

She, rather.

Rowan's hands opened and flew up in the air, heed-less of bow and arrow dropping to the ground. "Etty!" she cried.

Two

Hugging Rowan around the neck, Etty teased, "If you didn't know *me*, you might at least recognize Dove."

The pony grazing close at hand, Etty meant. Just a white pony in an ordinary brown leather bridle and saddle, with none of the fancy plumes and trappings once worn by the mount of the king's page boy; how was Rowan supposed to know Dove from any other white pony? Confound that teasing Etty, she knew very well that all horses looked alike to Rowan, with a front end that bit and a hind end that kicked and a stinky middle to fall off of.

But Rowan couldn't retort properly. She was crying.

Ettarde let her go and looked her up and down, still teasing, although her perfect symmetrical face under the visorless helm looked as sober as an egg. "You have bosoms, Ro. Finally!"

Ro still couldn't respond, although she tried to smile.

The mischief blinked out of Etty's gray-green eyes. "Ro, is something wrong?"

Rowan found her voice. "I don't know. Not with you." Knuckling the tears out of her eyes so that she could see Etty properly, Rowan thought that her friend looked well. Not happy, necessarily, and not un-changed, but strong. Perhaps it had been necessary for Ettarde to grow even stronger than before, surviving as an outsider in her uncle's castle.

Etty demanded, "Are your legs still hurting you?"

"Yes, but—"

Tykell growled.

Both girls stiffened, scanning and listening. They saw nothing yet, but in a moment they heard the ap-proaching danger: hooves, many hooves, drumming in the distance. Horseback riders on the Nottingham Way.

"Take cover." Grabbing her bow and arrows, Rowan fled toward the forest, trying to run. But up the waste-land's rocky slope, the best she could manage was a limping trot.

"Get on Dove," Etty urged, trotting alongside Rowan with Ro's bag of coltsfoot in one hand, Dove's reins in the other.

"That would take me even longer."

"But . . ." Etty did not complete the thought, only flung the reins over Dove's head so that they lay on the pony's neck, then whacked Dove with the bag of colts-foot. Startled, Dove sprang away and galloped off, saddle and bridle and baggage and all, into the forest. As always when anything ran away, Tykell let out a joyous "Wuff!" and bounded after. In a moment both pony and wolf-dog had disappeared between the trees.

What in the Lady's name—but there was no time for Rowan to yell at Tykell to stop, demand of Etty whether she had gone moon mad, or do anything except totter onward, her legs aching and shaking. Somehow she had to make it to the bushes and hide before the men on horseback rounded the curve in the Nottingham Way and saw her. It might already be too late.

Etty seemed to judge that it was. "Down!" she commanded in a whisper, pushing Rowan to the ground. Finding herself suddenly flat on her belly, Rowan let bad enough alone, kept her head close to the ground and stayed still. Inches from her, Etty also sprawled on heather and stones, snatching off her shiny helm; her long dark hair coiled out from under it. She slid the helm under Rowan's brown mantle. Hidden only by the bare dun stems of last year's furze, both girls froze like rabbits, watching as the horsemen rode into sight.

Led by two knights in full chain-mail armor, lances in the air, a cavalcade of eight men-at-arms advanced, the soldiers' russet tabards cross-girded with black to form an X across their chests. They raised no dust at this moist time of year; Rowan could see them clearly. The same device, a black X, was blazoned on the knights' shields and the pennons that fluttered like small pointed flags from their lance shafts.

"The mark of Marcus," said Etty, for there was no fear of being overheard by the men trotting along in a cloud not of dust, but of their own noise: hooves on stone, saddles creaking, weapons and armor jingling, voices. "Those are my uncle's men." Etty's serene voice sounded as surprised as Rowan had ever heard it. "I hadn't thought they could be so close behind me."

Any man of Marcus who gave a glance upward might see Rowan and Etty only half hidden by the crest of the slope, two outlaw girls pretending to be brown boulders amid rocks, gorse bushes and coltsfoot.

Barely moving her lips, and not moving any other part of her at all, Rowan asked Etty, "You ran away?"

"Of course."

"Why of course? They mistreated you?"

"No, not at all. It is just that my uncle cannot conceive of a girl or woman free to come and go."

"Then your mother—"

"He still thinks of her as his little sister. To be protected."

"So she has no freedom."

"No. But she never did, except those few days . . ."

During the brief time spent with her daughter in Sherwood Forest, Ettarde's mother—queen of the kingdom of Auberon—had relished freedom, Rowan knew.

"She doesn't miss it?"

"I don't know. She would never say so."

"Is she happy?"

"She is . . . brave. Mother was always determined to be content with her lot. And proud. She refuses to wear black."

Black?

The black gown and veil of a widow?

Eyes on the soldiers on horseback trotting toward Nottingham, careful not to move, Rowan kept silence a moment to control her reaction. Then she whispered, "Your father?"

"Dead."

"I—I'm sorry."

Etty did not speak. Rowan sensed that she could not speak, or not with safety, not without making some movement that might betray them. They lay silent, motionless.

Rowan let several moments go by before she murmured, "Does your mother know where you are?"

"Yes, in a general way. But not precisely."

This answer baffled Rowan. She tried again. "You told her where you were going?"

"I asked her whether she wanted to come along. She chose to stay behind, and she didn't want to have to lie to Uncle Marcus, so she wanted to know nothing more. I slipped away with her blessing."

"Oh." Rowan lay puzzling over the ways of noble families, wondering whether lovely Queen Elsinor was fond of her brother Marcus and whether Lord Marcus felt affection for her. And how Queen Elsinor could love Etty the way Rowan knew she did, yet could let her ride away. Finally Ro murmured, "You told her goodbye."

"Of course. I promised you I'd come back, Ro."

Etty's hand crouched as still as a hiding mouse amid coltsfoot in bloom near Rowan's face. On one finger lustered a serpentine strand of silver, a ring. One strand of the band. Others were worn by Rook, Lionel and Beau. The two remaining strands remained on Rowan's hand. Without looking, without moving, she could feel their presence on her ring finger. The gimmal ring, the six strands that formed one, had belonged to Rowan's mother before she died. Was killed, rather. Now the strands of Celandine's ring had become the emblem of a band. An outlaw band.

Yes, Rowan had expected that Ettarde would return sometime—but alone? Unescorted, in danger and in haste? Etty had ridden hard; Rowan had seen the sweat foaming and crusting on Dove's neck. Chest pressed to cold stones, Ro felt as if the air around her had also turned to stone. Her heart lay clay cold, and not with fear of Marcus's men, who were riding away.

"There's something else," she said to Etty without moving her head. "I've been feeling it all day."

Etty lay silent until the last rider had trotted past and the sound of hoofbeats and jingling harnesses had faded.

Rowan was a friend to silence, but this time she could not stand it. "Etty?"

"Wait till we can move."

When the backs of the riders had grown small with distance, disappearing around a bend in the road toward Nottingham, Rowan turned her head and said again, "Etty?"

But Ettarde didn't answer yet, just stood up. Even though she wore the heavy boots of a youth, Etty got to her feet gracefully, as befit a princess. Reaching down, she helped Rowan stand. But as Rowan faced her, Etty turned away, beckoning, walking toward the forest.

"Dove's too white," confided Ettarde, for all the world like a princess making court conversation. "Even in the bushes she shines like a full moon rising. There was no time to hide her, but we can track her and find her, I think, if Tykell hasn't chased her clear to—"

"*Etty*," Rowan interrupted.

Beneath the shelter of the first towering oak tree, Etty turned to face her.

Rowan whispered, "What is it that brought you back here, wearing a sword at your side?"

Ettarde took a deep breath, met Rowan's gaze with somewhat less than her usual composure, and answered. "I have learned the names of those who murdered your mother."

Three

The rowan trees had whispered truth that morning. Now, at nightfall, sitting in her accustomed place beside the spring, Rowan heard the rowan grove all around her rustling in the breeze, but she could no longer hear how the trees sighed *Good-bye, good-bye.* Resting her back against the concealing boulders, she heard the trickle of sweetwater in the stone bowl of the spring, but she could no longer hear its gentle grief as it bade her farewell. This morning she had sensed how the very stones, bones of Sherwood Forest, silently lamented of loss: *Farewell, Rowan, fare well.* But tonight she sensed nothing. Stones were only stone.

She gazed into the evening campfire but saw nothing except flames. The others around the campfire, eagerly talking with Etty as they ate their dinner of bread and venison, could not possibly know, but Rowan knew: Her body sat in the rowan hollow, but in spirit she had already departed. No longer at one with her rowan grove and its sweetwater spring, in a sense she was already gone.

I will come back, she had once whispered to another such spring far to the north: Celandine's spring. *I will come back someday, and I will find out the names of those who set their torches to the thatch, and they will pay. Somehow they will pay.*

Rowan Hood was gone, had been gone since the minute she had heard Etty's news. In her place lived a grieving girl Rowan had thought she had left behind: Rosemary, daughter of Celandine.

". . . hadn't been in that castle for half a day before one of Uncle Marcus's henchmen tried to back me into a corner and place his hands upon me," Etty was telling big, ardent Lionel and the others, explaining the sword she now wore. "I seized my quarterstaff and drubbed him till he fell down the stairs. Well! Such an uproar as ensued." Pausing to slice a neat bite from her portion of venison, Etty rolled her beautiful eyes. "A girl who *fought back?* Every day and *every* day after that some so-called knight had to have a go at me."

"But my dear little lady, how appalling!" Lionel leaned forward, his broad shoulders looming over her, his full-moon face distraught, his babyish mouth steepled in distress.

"I'm not your dear lady, little or otherwise," Etty told him tartly. But she smiled.

"My dear princess! Did your uncle not protect you?"

"Had one of his minions carried me off and ravished me," said Etty sourly, "surely my uncle would have found it necessary to avenge the family honor."

"Ettarde!"

"Or if a mere man-at-arms had tried to overcome me and force a kiss, it would have been a serious matter. But a knight, that is different. Might makes right, you know. Even though any jack-in-boots with a horse and armor can title himself a knight."

"Still, your uncle—"

"Is no worse than any other lord. He has to keep the loyalty of his henchmen."

"So he let them force themselves on you. My dear princess, did any of them *succeed*?"

"Not a one."

"*Mon foi*, good for you!" exclaimed another voice: Beau, sitting atop the rocks with her head resting against Dove's neck, her black hair flowing at one with Dove's white mane. Beau had wept for joy, taking possession once again of the pony that had been hers. She would have brought Dove right into the grove if she could have maneuvered the little horse over the surrounding natural rock wall. But even hugging Dove could not keep Beau silent for long. *"Très bon,"* she told Etty. "Well done."

"So then, you see, one of them drew his sword upon me, and I wrested it away and started wearing it."

"Most dreadful," Lionel complained.

"The company was not pleasant," Etty admitted. "At first I spent my days closeted, doing needlework." Etty made a droll face to indicate that she had not much enjoyed embroidering wimples. "With my mother, to comfort her."

Rowan wanted to ask more about Queen Elsinor: whether her husband, returning to his petty kingdom, had ever begged her forgiveness, and how she had learned of his fate. But Rowan could not speak; it was as if the air around her had bruised and swollen to hold her silent.

"Later," Etty went on, "I began visiting the dungeons."

"What?" Lionel cried.

"Sacre bleu!" exclaimed Beau.

Rook asked, "Why?"

Etty beamed at him. "Rook, you haven't changed so very much." Even though she had barely recognized him at first with his black hair smooth and clean, the rest of him clean and dressed in shoes and sheepskin leggings and a jerkin Beau had dyed rusty red for him. "You still speak short words straight to the point."

He said nothing, but he smiled. Likely, Rowan thought, never until that day had Etty seen Rook smile. But her heart ached too much to allow her joy in the thought.

Lionel asked Etty, "You went to take food to the prisoners?"

Trust Lionel to think first of food, Rowan thought, but again she could not smile.

"Sometimes, yes," Etty said, "although my uncle Marcus is not unkind to his captives. Chiefly, I went to the dungeons because no one would think to look for me there, and because men behind bars could not attempt to put their hands upon me. Perforce they had to talk with me instead. Later, after I had won some of them over, they instructed me in the use of this." She tapped the sword lying close beside her.

"Oh," said Lionel, his mouth an O, round.

"And I whiled away much time by listening to their conversation among themselves. Most of them had been captured when their lord, Orric of Borea, had tried to invade my uncle's domain. They were knights being held for ransom, or to keep them from turning their swords against my uncle again, or both. Generally they bragged of feats of combat, and excuses to challenge one another, as if fighting and killing were fun. You know the sort, Lionel."

He grimaced, presumably remembering his days as Lord Roderick's son. "I know all too well."

"But sometimes they spoke of their families, their homes in Borea, things that had happened there. And then came a day I heard one of them mention Celandine's Wood, and I asked whether they knew aught of the woodwife Celandine."

Pushing her dinner aside, Etty leaned forward to lessen the distance between her and Rowan, her gray-green eyes consulting Ro across the width of the stone hollow. Rowan saw the question there.

"Go ahead and tell them," she answered aloud. She had already gathered the gist of the story from Etty during the day, piecemeal, as if gathering up the bones of her mother's dead body.

"I don't like to speak of it if it hurts you."

"But one of us has to." Those who wore the strands of Celandine's ring shared their troubles. What affected one of them affected all. "Better you."

So Etty spoke on. "They told me that four of Lord Orric's knights had ridden to Celandine's Wood, bearing torches in the daytime. Torches not for light to see by, but torches for fire. To burn down the cottage of the one they hated and feared."

"Woods witch," the castle folk had called Rowan's mother, disliking the power of woodsy magic and healing, power that had threatened their own. All dwellers in the forest—wolves, outlaws, the invisible spirits of trees and water, the ageless aelfe of the hollow hills, wild boars, wild men—all who dwelt in the forest gave uneasy dreams to Orric, Lord of Borea. Including—no, especially—the one whom the peasants called "the woodwife," practitioner in salves and herbs and spirit lore, the half-aelfin woman who cottaged with her wild brat of a bastard daughter in the wilderness the common folk called "Celandine's Wood." Naming the place in the witch's honor, as if she were of the nobility.

Etty was saying, "So, pretending a lazy sort of curiosity, I asked Orric's men who the four knights were who had done this deed. And they named them to me."

Ettarde, scholar that she was, had written down the names on a vellum she had rolled and thrust down her tunic, carrying it over her heart. Rowan, who knew nothing of reading or writing, had no need of such a scroll. The first moment Etty had read them to her, those names had branded themselves in her memory:

Guy Longhead.

Jasper of the Sinister Hand.

Hurst Orricson.

Holt, also Orricson, brother of Hurst.

Orricson—that meant "Orric's son." The lord's sons.

"Orric's henchmen whispered the names as if it

23

would be ill luck to speak them aloud," Ettarde was telling the others. "And even though these were warriors, supposedly braver than peasants, still, they made the sign of the Lady as if they feared a curse. Then they fell silent and would say no more."

A similar silence fell on those seated around the campfire. In that silence Rowan could hear nothing of the soft voices that usually spoke to her, only a scream somewhere in the forest night; a mouse caught in the talons of an owl that had swooped down as silently as a ghost?

Rowan shivered, then got up to place more wood on the campfire. It seemed to her sometimes that she was always the one who saw to the fire, the one who took care of the others. Muttonheads, why couldn't *they* notice sometimes when the flames were dying? Kneeling, Rowan started to whisper thanks to the spirit of fire as she usually did, then faltered to a halt. The sticks fell from her hands.

"Are you all right?" Etty asked.

Rowan heard her friend's voice as if from a distance, like the rustling of bracken as deer walked. At first she did not respond. But again as if from a distance she felt them all staring at her, big softhearted Lionel, Etty, Rook, Beau—even Tykell, the wolf-dog, looked at her as if waiting for her to speak.

Rowan muttered, "Fire killed my mother."

After a single breath of silence, the others spoke too quickly. *"Mon Dieu,* not *this* fire," said Beau.

Lionel burst out, "But my dear Rowan, evil *men* killed your mother with fire. It's they who are to blame, not the . . ."

"It's my fault for telling you," Etty said. "I should have let ill enough alone."

Rook alone remained silent. Instead of speaking, he reached over to pick up the sticks Rowan had dropped, but he did not feed them to the fire. He stacked them to one side.

"Mother told me not to meddle." Etty's voice sounded stretched and hollow, like a drum. "She said it would be kinder to let you forget—"

"I'd never forget!" Rowan's voice beat taut like a drum too—a battle drum. "My mother is dead." Celandine the healer, Celandine the good, Celandine the flower of the woodland, cut down. Burned. Dead. "I am going back there."

The words seemed to hover over the fire like a red specter, with everyone, even Rowan, staring at them. She had not planned to speak them; it was as if her mind were wounded and the words had bled out of it.

But they were true.

"I have to go back," Rowan affirmed more quietly.

"Rowan, don't be hasty." Etty lifted a dove-white hand, appealing, "Wait a day or two. Sleep on it."

Rowan just looked at her good friend. Couldn't even shake her head. It was as if a padlock had snapped shut in her. "I can't wait," she said. "But you don't need to come with me if you don't want to, any of you. I—"

"*Sacre amour* of the toad, Rowan," Beau burst out, "you talk stupid!"

"Of course we'll go with you," Lionel complained. "If you *must* go. It shouldn't take longer than, what, a year?"

Etty put all her plea in a single word. "Rowan . . ."

Rowan still heard her as if from a distance. And in the same way, she heard Rook's gruff voice speak up. "Whether you go or not, your mother will still be dead."

Rook spoke good common sense, always.

But Rowan shook her head. "The four who set their torches to the thatch remain alive. And I know their names now." Once again it was as if words issued out of her like blood from a wound. "It is up to me to make them pay."

She reached for the sticks Rook had set aside and she fed them to the fire.

Four

Sleep on it, Etty had kept saying.

But Rowan couldn't sleep.

At the chillest hour of night, when even the embers of the fire huddled dark under a gray blanket of ashes, Rowan softly pushed back her own blanket of wool and stood up, silent in her soft deerskin boots. She had dozed only a little, and then her dreams had been of huge, shadowy stallions fighting. On her feet now, Rowan breathed deeply the good brown-green smells of Sherwood Forest, hearing with relief the quiet sounds of night: twigs ticking, her comrades in the rowan hollow stirring as they slept, rock doves murmuring in the tall oaks that stretched their branches, fatherly, over the shorter rowans.

Father, Rowan thought.

She needed to speak with him. Tell him where she was

going. Maybe *he,* at least, would understand. Robin Hood, outlaw and many times the avenger of the innocent—maybe he would see why she had to return to where her mother had died. No one in the band seemed to comprehend. Not Rook on his favorite sheepskin, curled in a corner of the hollow tonight instead of in his cave. Not Lionel, sitting like a monolith atop the rocks, upright yet asleep, snoring when he was supposed to be on watch. Not Beau, her blanket in a mess and her long limbs wildly sprawling, or Etty, tidily bestowed within her mantle's wrappings, the perfect lady even in repose. Etty, after having risked her uncle's wrath to bring Rowan those four names, understood perhaps least of all.

What did she expect me to do?

But Rowan did not question her own decision. What troubled Rowan was the dark emptiness inside her where her heart should have been. Was this the way vengeance always felt?

Picking up her bow and her quiver of arrows, she slipped silently out of the hollow. Lionel snored on. The big oaf, she should have snapped him on the ear with her fingernail, but she let him slumber. No one saw her go. Not even Tykell, for at nighttime the wolf-dog hunted on his own, and Lady only knew where in Sherwood Forest he had gone.

Sliding her feet rather than lifting them, testing the

ground, step by silent step Rowan walked into the darkness on her own.

She did not feel afraid. Not yet. In the distance she heard the hunting song of a pack of wolves chasing deer. She had feared wolves when she had been a little girl sleeping near her mother's hearth, but now she was herself a forest dweller and she feared them no more. Twigs brushed her face, not always gently, not too much like a mother's touch, but they were just the forest fingertips of the Lady, nothing to fear.

Rowan felt her way across familiar ground, out of the rowans and through the oaks, then upslope between hemlock and holly, turning her mind this way and that like a red deer turning its head as it tested the air for scent.

Father? Rowan questioned the night, seeking with her mind in every direction.

But she sensed no answer.

The forest, like the rowans and the sweetwater spring, was not speaking to her anymore.

Now Rowan felt fear.

Father?

Still she could not feel his whereness.

It could just be a vexed night, a troubled mind, Rowan told herself. Powers were quirky in her. All such gifts, legacy of her mother's aelfin blood, had bloomed in her late and slowly because she had been—well, afraid.

Afraid that she would become a woodwife like her mother.

Afraid that she would live her life alone. Like her mother.

Afraid that some lord's henchmen on horseback would come to kill her. As Lord Orric's henchmen had killed her mother.

Now she had become an outlaw, not a woodwife, and she was not living her life alone. During two years in her rowan hollow with her outlaw band, her powers had waxed like a crescent moon growing full, while her fears had waned like a decrescent one, almost forgotten. But now—this was a shrouded night, no moon, no stars, and Rowan began to feel those old fears twitching in their sleep, awakening to join a new one: that something was wrong with her, that she couldn't—

No. Don't even think "couldn't."

"Toads and stinky toads," Rowan muttered to herself. Given the perverse way her powers flooded and ebbed, she would get nowhere, trying to find her father, if she doubted herself or tried too hard. Also, she muttered of toads because her legs hurt. They always hurt where they had been broken in the man trap two winters ago, for there had been no healer to help them knit properly.

Perverse, again, that the healer could not heal herself.

Sighing, Rowan sat down where she was, upslope of the hemlocks. Black night was turning faintly gray with the twilight of earliest morning, before dawn, before daybreak. Nottingham Way wound like a pale stream amid the darker forest below, widening into a ghostly pool, a clearing, Fountain Dale, upon which floated little dark boats.

As dawn lightened, the little boats grew slender legs and turned into deer, fallow deer drifting toward the verge of Fountain Dale to disappear into their thickets for the day.

Rowan closed her eyes, listening to the gentle overlapping rhythms of her own heartbeat and breathing, waiting for fear to ebb in her and calm to return. She did not want to return to the rowan hollow and face the others until she felt steady in her resolve. She would just sit with her eyes closed for a few minutes.

"Seize her!" shouted a commanding voice close at hand.

Rowan's eyes sprang open and her head snapped up—much too late. Daylight blinded her; already the sun had risen into the treetops. All was a confusion of sunbeams and shadows and hands—hard hands that sprang out of hemlock and holly to grasp her by the arms, hauling her to her feet. More hands grabbed hold of her wrists, giving her no chance to snatch for her bow, her arrows, her dagger. Strong warrior hands. Rowan fought to break free, flailing and squirming like a trapped ferret. But it was no use. Like a fool she had fallen asleep, and now she had been fairly taken off guard.

Men-at-arms on foot surrounded her, so tall that she blinked not at their faces, but at their strong chests, their tabards bound shoulder to waist with black sashes that formed an X.

"Where is Princess Ettarde?" demanded the commanding voice.

Blinking, still trying to understand what was happening, Rowan did not answer.

The captain roared, "Speak up, outlaw girl, or you'll feel the flat of my hand across your face! Where is Princess Ettarde?"

Oh. They were Lord Marcus's men. Looking for Etty. Pure stubbornness on the part of Lord Marcus, as Etty was hardly worth retaking; she was now a princess in name only. Her father's petty kingdom had indeed fallen to Lord Basil, Etty had told Ro, and her father had met death more honorably than anyone could have expected. Rather than letting his people's blood be shed, King Solon—the scholar who could barely lift a sword—had himself defied Lord Basil at the gates, and had been killed.

Thinking this, thinking of how Etty had almost cried as she had spoken of it, Rowan gawked up at her captors, wordless.

"The girl's no outlaw, dozing in the sun," said another man's voice. "She's a simpleton. A beggar, belike, or a goose girl."

"A goose girl with a bow and peacock-feathered arrows?" retorted the leader. "And a kirtle of Lincoln green, and deerskin boots?"

"But look at her lackwit eyes. This can't be Rowan Hood. Perhaps this simpleton stole the —"

Hooves drummed on the rocky slope above their heads. The men's hands jumped on Rowan's arms as they startled, all of them turning and kinking their necks to look.

About an arrow's flight away, a white pony trotted into sight on the crest of the rocky scarp. On the pony rode a lovely—girl, in her belted tunic unmistakably a girl, even though upon her head she wore a shining half-helm.

Rowan felt her eyes widen and her jaw drop in a manner appropriate to a lackwit. She almost shouted the girl's name out loud: *Ettarde!*

"Princess!" bellowed the captain.

The runaway princess halted Dove. A grotesquely hued garment was that tunic she wore, mottled purplish-brown—the color of an engorged flea, actually. One of Beau's masterpieces. Now that Beau was no longer forced to wear "black and black and *toujours* black," the bumptious girl "adored to *couleur*" clothing such as this unfortunate tunic. But Ettarde wore the unlovely thing with the dignity of a true princess. From her pony's saddle she scanned her uncle's men with her usual tranquility.

The captain bellowed, "Princess, I order you to—"

Etty did not await her orders. Without a word she wheeled the pony and cantered out of sight over the hilltop.

"To horse!" roared the captain. "After her!"

All the hands clutching Rowan fell away so suddenly that her arms felt curiously light, lifting like wings. She found herself standing alone while a great deal of crashing and rattling ensued in the hemlock grove to either side of her: the men-at-arms struggling to locate their concealed horses, untether them and mount them.

From somewhere close at hand a low, gruff voice said, "Rowan, come on."

Rook?

Dazedly Rowan glanced around, looking for him, but just then half a dozen men on horseback burst out of the hemlocks and galloped up the hill after Etty, with the shouting captain in the lead.

The horses lunged, hooves clawing at the steep slope, spraying dirt and gravel. But once they got to the top . . . These steeds were far larger, longer of leg than the pony Etty rode.

Marcus's soldiers must not catch her!

Do something.

Rowan snatched for her bow.

"Cuckoo in your nest, get out of *sight*," said the voice that sounded like Rook's, although for him "cuckoo in your nest" was overspending of speech.

Ignoring him, Rowan struggled to nock an arrow to the bowstring.

A wolfish roar made her jump, dropping the arrow. Gawking, Rowan saw a large comet of gray-brown fur fly out from between the oaks at the top of the rise, cutting off the cavalcade, launching itself toothily at the first horse's big pink nose.

The horse shrieked and reared.

"Tykell!" Rowan screamed at the same time.

Straight up in the air to save its tender nostrils, the horse dumped its rider, then fell over backward, almost on top of him. Belly floundering, hooves flailing, it struggled to regain its footing on the slope. The other horses swirled and plunged; their riders shouted, trying to control their mounts and at the same time draw their swords. Tykell lunged again—

And Rowan saw no more, for someone very large and strong picked her up, bow and arrows and all, whisking her off in the opposite direction, into the cover of the hemlocks.

"Lionel, let me go!" Once before, when the Sheriff of Nottingham's men had roped her arms to her sides, wrapping her like a bobbin, Rowan had been carried off bodily by Lionel, and that had been one time too many. "Tykell—"

"You know Ty can take care of himself." Cradling her effortlessly in his arms, Lionel strode on.

"Put me *down*!"

Lionel merely lengthened his stride.

But not in the right direction, Rowan thought. She squirmed, fighting his grip. "Where are you going? We have to help *Etty*."

"Dolt, Etty's helping *you*," said Rook's gritty voice from somewhere near Lionel's elbow.

"I'm right here," said another voice, the dulcet voice of a princess. Without rustling so much as a single twig, Etty emerged from the brush to join them.

Five

Why, Ettarde, my dear little princess." Lionel halted, set Rowan on her feet and gave Etty an exaggerated bow, sweeping off an imaginary hat to greet her. "Fancy meeting you in such an out-of-the-way—"

"Hush, buffoon." Not even bothering to scowl at Lionel, Etty instead gave Rowan her most placid smile. She still wore her oddly colored tunic, but what had become of her helm? Her brown hair streamed down around her shoulders.

Rowan blinked and shook her head, feeling unsteady on her feet for some reason. "What's going on?"

"I jumped off Dove and gave Beau my helm," Etty explained with quiet enjoyment. "She—"

"Keep moving," growled Rook, several paces ahead of the rest of them, looking back over his shoulder. There was no fear that Lord Marcus's men-at-arms would hear them talking; the soldiers were making a great deal of noise on their own account, and that commotion was already fading far behind. Still, Rook looked not nearly as tranquil as Etty.

"Goodness gracious, my dear little lad . . ." Lionel strode forward to join Rook. Rowan hitched herself into motion and walked, feeling stiff, limping.

Strolling beside Rowan, Etty continued her tale. "Beau jammed my helm onto her head, jumped onto Dove and galloped off while I slipped into the bushes. She'll lead my uncle's men in a merry chase. If they catch sight of her whatsoever, all they'll see is her white pony and her shiny helm and her tunic, and they'll think she's me. She was wearing another of these dreadful archil tunics—"

Trust Etty to know the correct name for the purplish color made with dye from lichens. And trust her to remember it even now.

Even though Beau was in peril.

Rowan blurted, "But what if they *catch* her?"

"They won't." Yet, like a roe deer testing the air for the scent or sound of danger, Ettarde lifted her elegant head and turned it from side to side, hearkening.

Rowan listened also, with dread in her heart. But she heard no one screaming, no one crying out. Only soft forest sounds. Only wagtail birds twittering, and a west wind soughing in the tall oak trees.

"Beau rides like a spirit of the wind," Etty added.

Rowan trudged on without answering.

"At the very worst," Etty said, "she will let Dove gallop onward while she climbs a tree. You know Beau climbs like a squirrel."

For one who sounded not at all concerned, Rowan thought, Etty was talking a great deal.

"Beau thought out the plan," Etty chatted on. "She told us where to meet her."

But what had happened to send them scheming and scrambling to help her, Rowan, while she slept? All of them Beau, Etty, Lionel, Rook, putting themselves in harm's way for her sake? Rowan felt—

From farther ahead Rook called, "Rowan." In his low voice, worry spoke plainer than it did in Etty's. "Rowan, can you walk faster?"

"Yes." Quickening her pace, Rowan managed a painful trot for a few moments, struggling to catch up with the others.

"My dear little lass," Lionel offered in his most cheerfully annoying courtly tone, "let me give you a lift."

Rowan felt like a useless fool. "Stop it, Lionel," she told him between clenched teeth. "I can *walk*."

But she couldn't.

Within the short span of what was left of the morning, she learned that she couldn't accomplish even such a simple thing as walking.

The sun bloomed like a golden flower never bowed by the wind, straight up in the apex of the sky; day had not even passed into afternoon, yet Rowan staggered as if battling her way through a stormy night. Perhaps for her sake, Rook and Lionel had led the way to the easiest ground in Sherwood, a grassy forest path made by deer along the soft bottom of a valley. And they had slowed the pace almost to a shuffle, glancing back over their shoulders at her. Yet Rowan could barely keep up.

With a "Wuff!" of greeting, Tykell trotted out of a thorn thicket to join Rowan, nosing her hand. Rowan felt something tighten like a bowstring inside her throat. Placing her hand on the wolf-dog's thickly furred back, she leaned sideward, resting her weight on Ty for a moment. Her aching legs—they had never felt this weak before.

Her friends stopped and watched her, waiting for her to move on, their silence bespeaking their worry for her more plainly than words.

Letting go of Ty, Rowan focused all the force of her

mind and will upon making her faltering legs move and walk. With her gaze fixed on the ground under her next step, then her next, then her next, she plodded on. If it had been just her legs that hurt—but it was more. Every inward fiber of her ached. *Mother. Dead. While those who had killed her still lived.* And it was even more than that. *There's something wrong with me.* Rowan's heart felt like a black hollow of misery.

Her toe caught on—nothing at all, nothing but flat grassy ground—and she fell sprawling, facedown, her breath knocked out.

Biting her lip to keep from crying like an overgrown baby, Rowan lay still for a moment too long. Before she could struggle to her feet, strong arms lifted her up, but did not set her on her feet. The big lummox was carrying her again.

"Lionel," ordered Rowan wearily, "put me down."

Without a word he strode onward, cradling her in his arms. Without a word Rook trotted by Lionel's left elbow, and Etty by his right. Tykell swished away into the brush on some errand of his own.

"I can walk," Rowan insisted.

"But I beg to differ. It's quite evident that you can't," said Lionel with none of his usual petulance. His low voice sounded almost grim. "What's wrong, Rowan?"

"I . . ." She had to close her eyes. "I don't know."

"But you must have *some* idea," he said, annoying as usual again, "my dear little girl—"

A blaze of anger jolted Rowan with welcome strength. She squirmed, trying to free herself from Lionel's arms; he was forced to slow down a bit to keep hold of her. "If you *ever* call me 'dear little girl' again," she told him between clenched teeth, "I will shave every curly hair off your parlous fat head with Etty's sword."

With an odd catch in his voice, Lionel told her, "May that day come soon. My dear little girl."

Rowan lost track of the passing of time. Joggling along in Lionel's giant grip made her feel dizzy. She closed her eyes again and kept them closed. Perhaps she slept. When she opened her eyes again and looked around, day had moved on toward late afternoon, and Rowan recognized the familiar slope down which Lionel was carrying her. They were entering the hollow folk called Robin Hood's Dell.

"What are we going here for?" Rowan demanded.

"For my hands to cramp and my arms to ache from hauling you," Lionel retorted in his best babyish whine, although he strode along as easily as ever.

"No, I mean, why *here*?" This time it was strength of panic that helped Rowan wriggle in his grip, almost sitting up straight.

"Hold still," Lionel complained. "What are you trying to do, pull my shoulders entirely out of their sockets?"

Etty's voice floated to Rowan. "We're going here to meet Beau, Ro. So that she could hide Dove entirely, do you see? Very clever—"

But Rowan barely heard, struggling wildly against Lionel's grip. "Put me down!"

"But, my dear Rowan—" Lionel sounded not peevish at all, only puzzled. And upset.

The big, stupid oaf. Rowan flared at him, "What if my father is here?" At the bottom of this hollow, in a clearing created by its own great expanse of branches, stood Robin Hood's giant oak tree. His favorite hideout. If he had happened to choose to spend this night here . . . "I don't want him to see me like this! Put me down!"

Oddly silent now, Lionel stopped and set her on her feet. Feeling a bit light-headed—perhaps because she hadn't eaten today, Rowan told herself—she stood blinking for a moment. But she saw the troubled looks Etty and Rook and Lionel exchanged.

Rook, straightforward as usual, spoke. "Wouldn't you know if Robin were here?"

"I—" Rowan shook her head, turned away. "Just let me alone," she mumbled, stumbling downhill toward the clearing.

Please, Rowan begged the spirits of the forest, *let my father be here.*

She should have been able to sense the oak lord as she passed an oak, the elm lady as she passed an elm, the sprites of ferns and wildflowers, and everywhere the ancient, ageless woodland dwellers, the aelfe.

But Rowan sensed no presences and no answer to her plea as she blundered down the slope between hornbeams and hazel bushes.

She could not even sense the presence of the prince of outlaws, he who was at one with this oak dell as Rowan had been at one with the rowan grove.

And indeed, when Rowan hobbled to the edge of the clearing, she found only fading, canted sundown light there. And Tykell, panting a black-lipped grin at her. And Beau, helm and archil tunic and all, perched on a low branch of the great oak, smiling at her.

Rowan couldn't smile.

Six

*V*_{*oilà!*} *Voulez-vous,* the Dove nest in the tree." Chattering her Frankish nonsense, gesturing, Beau led Rowan and the others inside the hollow oak. Sure enough, Rowan saw, the girl had hidden the pony inside Robin's tree; nowhere else in Sherwood Forest could Dove's white form have been so completely concealed. "The big *bête* Lionel, he take up more room than Dove," Beau teased, "but somehow we all fit in."

The minute she pushed through the concealing brush and limped inside the opening at the back of the oak, Rowan folded to a seat on the loamy ground, leaning against the corklike innards of the great tree. With her head tilted back, she closed her eyes.

"Rowan?" Etty's voice.

Rowan opened her eyes. Yes, they had all fit into the tree—Etty, Lionel, Rook, Beau, Tykell and Dove—and with the exception of the pony, they were all looking at her. Even in the dim twilight inside the oak she could feel their questioning stares.

"Ro, what is the matter with you?" Etty asked.

Rowan felt a noose of misery choke her throat again. She turned her face away from the question.

"Bah." The growl came from Rook. "Food first. Talk later. Here." Reaching into his jerkin, he pulled out a packet and tossed it to Lionel. He flung one to Beau, also, and one to Etty, but he leaned over to place Rowan's in her hands. Then he pulled out one more for himself, settled back on his haunches and tore it open.

"But—but—" Undoing the rag of muslin that enfolded his portion, Lionel nearly babbled with excitement. "But this is cheese! Heavenly yellow cheese and barley bread and—by my beard, dried apples!"

"You don't have a beard," Etty said. "Dried pears, I think."

"Apples, pears, I care not, *where* did it come from?"

"While my uncle's men were bullying Rowan, Rook robbed their horses' saddlebags, of course." Etty stated this as if she had expected nothing less. "Thank you, Rook."

He actually replied. "You're welcome."

Cheese, bread and fruit were a treat for any outlaw;

the usual fare in Sherwood Forest was meat, meat and more meat. Nibbling at the good food, Rowan felt sick with hunger, yet had to force herself to chew and swallow. After eating less than half her portion, Rowan sighed, pushed the rest away and leaned back.

"Don't you want that?" Lionel asked.

There was a ripple of laughter, and even Rowan almost smiled, feeling a bit better now that she'd eaten. Trust Lionel to beg for food. "Toads have laid their eggs in it," she told him.

"Ew!" But then, rather doubtfully Lionel inquired, "May I have it anyway?"

Etty picked up a bit of wood and tossed it at Lionel's head.

"Ow!" he complained, although the chip had hit him with all the force of a feather.

"For the love of mercy, Lionel, hush." In the near-darkness within the hollow oak, Rowan could feel Etty studying her. "Rowan," the outlaw princess demanded—softly, but with authority to command— "what's wrong?"

Silence. Listening for the forest to help her answer, Rowan heard the distant nightfall song of a thrush, but she could not hear the breathing of the oak within which she sat, or feel its embrace.

She felt only the patience of her friends waiting for an answer. Which was all she could give them.

Although feeling not quite as numb and heavy as the night before, Rowan still had to struggle to speak. Slowly she told them, "I think—I think I'm not Rowan anymore."

Silence cried out for a moment before Rook asked in his matter-of-fact way, "If not Rowan, then who are you?"

"I think—I'm just Rosemary."

Again silence screamed. Again it was Rook who spoke. "Why?"

"I don't—I can't hear the stones breathing anymore. This oak"—Rowan touched the ridgy inner wood against which she leaned—"it's just an oak, it doesn't welcome me. I felt no spirit in any tree I encountered today, or in running water, or in ferns, flowers, air, sky, anything."

Silence, in which Rowan felt their stares. In the hush of dusk, a nightingale added its song to that of the thrush.

"At the rowan grove, I can't converse with the spring." Rowan leaned toward the others, laboring to explain, her words faltering much as her feet had been stumbling all day. "The rowans said good-bye to me, and since then, they haven't spoken to me at all."

Rook asked, "When was this?"

"Yesterday."

Etty pressed her lips together into a line like a knife blade. "I knew it," she said, bleak and stark. "I brought it on you somehow. I shouldn't have—"

"Mischance is no one's fault." Beau, usually the loquacious one, had been silent for so long that everyone turned toward the sound of her voice as she quoted, " 'Welcome the stormwind of the soul, for it sweeps all clean and prepares it for a new day's sunrise.' Marcus Aurelius."

Etty's eyes widened. "I don't remember that in Marcus Aurelius."

"So, maybe it was Cicero. *Peu importe;* no matter. We need a fire."

"We need music." Lionel reached for the bag in which he kept his harp.

Both Lionel and Beau were trying to offer the same thing: comfort.

Rook, however, bespoke the hard thing that Ro had not yet mentioned. "You can't tell where Robin is."

Ro's eyes filled with tears, but she sobbed only once before she checked herself.

She did not need to answer. That small sound had answered for her.

Without a word, Beau struck her steel dagger blade

with a shard of flint she carried for that purpose. She struck again, with a chuffing sound, and again, making sparks fly in a bright shower to sprinkle a handful of pulpy tinder. She did not stop until tiny flames sprouted from the dry, powdery wood.

Rowan could see the others now, or at least their faces hovering in the firelight like four tawny oval moons.

Eyes on the flames, Etty murmured, "Well thought, Beau. It's safe enough, a campfire in here, if we don't let it get too big."

"Like me, perhaps?" Lionel inquired.

No one answered the joke.

Rook said, "Rowan."

Not just Rowan looked to him; they all did. When Rook spoke at all, he spoke like an arrow to the mark, always.

Rook said, "What you have lost is nothing any of us need to survive. Beau cannot see spirits. I cannot converse with trees. Ettarde cannot find hidden water. Lionel cannot tell where his father is."

Rowan thought about that for a moment, then mumbled, "I see."

"See what?" Etty asked. "I don't."

"That I'm being a crybaby. It is no loss for me to be like the rest of you."

"But it is loss! You are part aelfin—"

"Bah." Rook's gruff voice took over again. "Speak no more of spirits. What use are spirits when she can't even walk?"

Somehow the weakness in her legs seemed to Rowan of less importance than the hollow in her heart. Yet Rook was right. An outlaw could live without seeing the faces of the aelfe in the mists that rose between the oak trees, but no outlaw could live without walking.

"My legs are much worse today," Rowan admitted. Somehow she was able to speak more easily now. "I don't know why."

"You're all but crippled," Rook said.

No one else spoke, but Rowan knew well enough what they were thinking: that a tall man striding a straight line through the forest would take two weeks or more to reach Celandine's Wood from here. Longer, if he needed to hunt and forage food to eat. A full cycle of the moon. That was how long it had taken Rowan to make the journey from Celandine's Wood to Sherwood Forest. Two years ago, when she still had strong legs.

Softly Lionel strummed his harp, its honey-golden notes melting into the bitter night, sweetening it. Etty laid sticks on the fire. Blossoming no bigger than a damask rose, it sent a dusting of pale yellow light onto the faces all around it. Sober faces.

Lionel said, "You can still go to Celandine's Wood. I'll carry you."

"No. That's ridiculous."

"It is not. I—"

"La, do not like fools argue," Beau broke in, Frankish accent rampant. "The little Dove, she will carry Rowan."

"Toads," Rowan murmured. She hated riding horses. The only times she had tried, she had fallen off and fallen off. Still—

Etty said, "But Dove is too white. Riding her is like riding a target."

"So? I dye her." Beau grinned. "With the lichens, aubergine, yes?"

A purple pony? Lionel threw back his big head and laughed. Etty laughed. Even Rowan had to smile.

Beau elaborated, "Or yellow, with the wild onions. I put her in the big, big pot and boil her—"

Rook said, "Put soot on the horse."

"*Mon foi,* that is too simple."

It *was* simple. Rowan sat up straighter, thinking. Yes, she could ride the pony if she had to. And Beau would go wherever Dove went, and Lionel had already made it plain that he planned to accompany Rowan.

Rowan looked to another old friend. "Etty, what will you do?" she asked.

"Walk alongside, of course."

"With your uncle's men after you?"

"They won't look for me to the north. Why would I run back toward my uncle's domain?"

Rook said, "They're looking for her at the grove."

Rowan's eyes widened.

"At first light, up they came through Fountain Dale."

"They found the *grove*?"

Rook nodded.

Odd, Rowan thought, that her heart should ache, when she did not mean to go back to the rowan grove anyway.

Rook said, "They got close before Lionel saw them coming." No wonder, Ro thought, as the clodpole had been asleep when she had left. But she hadn't the heart to rebuke him, and apparently no one else did either. Rook was saying, "We got out with what we could snatch up and carry, nothing more."

Dully Rowan considered what had been left behind—blankets, cooking gear, supplies. But what matter, when even the grove and the spring did not seem to matter anymore? After a minute she said slowly, "So none of us would be safe there anyway. It was meant to be. We'll go north to—"

Etty interrupted, her usually placid voice fierce. "To do what, Rowan?"

Lionel's hand slipped and struck a discordant note. Quickly he stilled his harp.

Silence. For a moment Rowan could not answer. But then she said, "Guy Longhead. Jasper of the Sinister Hand. Hurst Orricson and his brother Holt." The names flamed in her mind and in her voice.

"What do you plan to do to them, Rowan? What *can* you do to them?"

"I don't know. But I'm going."

"I'll go with you anywhere, Ro. But I will not help you murder—"

"Vengeance is not murder!" Rowan curled her fists. "Mine is the blood right under—"

"Under the code of knights, so that they may never lack an enemy with whom to fight for the sake of so-called honor—"

"No! I am saying, mine is the right under the common law."

"The same law that has made us outlaws?"

Beau whispered, "I will not do killing in cold blood." In the firelight her dark eyes looked huge, like shadowed moons.

Lionel appealed, "Surely it will not come to that."

"I have known what it is to crave vengeance," said

Rook, his tone toneless, neutral. "So have you, Princess Ettarde."

"I am going back to my mother's woods," Rowan told her friends through clenched teeth. "I am going *home*. With you if I may. Without you if I must. Even if my legs fail me. Even if I have to crawl."

Seven

S urely we will encounter Robin somewhere along the way," Lionel told Rowan softly as he lifted her onto the pony.

In Dove's saddle, Ro turned to find her face on a level with Lionel's. It felt odd not to look up at him. It felt odd to be seated on a pony, any pony, let alone one rubbed gray all over with charcoal from last night's campfire. It felt odd to see Robin Hood's Dell without Robin Hood in it. It felt odd to look at hazel bushes and oak saplings and fair linden trees that did not look back. It felt odd to be leaving.

Everything felt odd.

But Rowan nodded at Lionel. It was true; surely on their journey they would at least hear word of Robin Hood from some peasant or forest recluse or traveler met along the way.

"Fare well and safely," Lionel told her. Picking up his longbow in one hand and his six-foot staff in the other, he strode off northward with his quiver of arrows on his back. Ranging ahead of the rest of them, he would scout for danger while trying to shoot something, perhaps a deer, for supper.

Beau slipped out of the hollow oak to stand by Rowan's side, silent for once, listening, waiting.

From the northeast lip of the hollow came the harsh call of a rook. A bit farther to the east sounded the whistle of a mistle thrush. Rook, the rook, was in position and ready. So was Etty, the mistle thrush.

Rowan trilled the warbling song of a wren in reply. Beau grinned up at her, silently telling her, *"Mon foi! You do that well."* Then Beau walked away. Rowan wondered how she was supposed to make Dove walk; lift the reins, or kick, or what? But no need. Dove followed Beau the way Tykell followed Rowan. There he was now, the wolf-dog, trotting in zigzags near her side.

Rook, who moved like a shadow in the forest, would be on the lookout for Marcus's men or any other danger. Etty, dressed in deerskin boots and a brown kirtle borrowed from Rowan, would do the same; in the woods she walked almost as silently as Rook. Beau would stay with Rowan and help her with the pony. And of course Tykell stayed with Rowan also, to protect her.

Rowan found it necessary to remind herself that she was an outlaw on a quest to avenge her mother's death. She didn't feel like much of an avenger. She felt worthless.

By the third day Rowan could tell herself that at least she had learned to balance on the pony and take charge of the reins. Necessarily so. On Dove's back, with her head at the height of Lionel's, Rowan encountered myriad sharp twigs that seemed determined to poke out her eyes, obstacles she needed to duck and steer clear of. Stout branches, also, seemed beset upon sweeping her off her mount. And grapevines, pesky things. If Rowan did not see them in time to push them aside, they caught like ropes around her waist. Once Rowan found herself dangling, head down above Dove's tail, before her grip on the reins halted the pony.

Never before had Rowan found herself so at war with the forest. She hated feeling that Sherwood had turned against her. She felt wretched.

Having never quite enough to eat did not help. Lionel shot meat, and Tykell, impatient with the slowness of Ro's pace, left her side to range about, sometimes bringing back a rabbit or two. Etty gathered greens, fennel and such. But there was little else to forage so early in the year.

Chill gray weather did not help either. It did not rain, but fog and damp shrouded the stark trees, and the sky stayed as gray as poor little Dove, covered with ashes.

And riding did not help—at first. But after a day or two of stiffness and sore muscles, Rowan learned to let her body sway along with the rhythm of the well-bred pony's pace, and then she found herself soothed, rocked as if in a mother's arms. Looking all day at Dove's ears, she found that they talked to her, fox-pricked alert, or angled with worry, or relaxed, or laid back in disapproval. But Dove seldom disapproved, almost always responding immediately to Rowan's gentlest tug on the reins. Ro learned gratitude to the patient pony who helped her struggle around and between the thorn thickets, the rustling bracken, the hanging grapevines. It was not Dove's fault that the oaks and beeches spread their branches too low, that sometimes Rowan had to lie flat, wrap her arms around Dove's neck and hide her face in Dove's soot-blackened mane to ride beneath the trees.

It was not Dove's fault, either, that human dangers threatened. Beau, like Rook and Etty and Lionel, carried a staff with which to test and probe the path, although there was less danger of man traps this early in the spring, when it was difficult for the foresters to conceal them. But the fewer the man traps, it seemed, the more the patrols. Half a dozen times a day the warning signal, a jay's cry, would come from Rook or Etty or both, and Beau would grab Dove's bridle and dart into the nearest thick shelter—evergreen, usually, hemlock or pine or holly or a scrim of ivy—and Rowan would hang on as Dove trotted after Beau, and the holly leaves or fir needles would claw her face. She would sit without moving in the saddle, and Beau would stand by Dove's head, stroking the pony's soft muzzle to keep her quiet, and they would wait to hear Rook or Etty give the cheery wagtail twitter that meant "all clear."

Usually they saw nothing, and only afterward would Etty tell them whether it had been foresters, or Nottingham's men, or Marcus's men still on the hunt for her. But once, they saw for themselves: bounty hunters, four rough-looking fellows on shaggy ponies, one with an outlaw's severed head hanging by the hair from the saddle. Rowan's heart turned over, for she knew that dead, hollow-eyed head. It had belonged to one of Robin's men.

After the bounty hunters had passed, Beau looked up at Rowan, her long Grecian-cameo face even whiter than usual. She whispered, "I can't remember his name."

Rowan shook her head. Robin Hood's band had grown to number close to a hundred men; she did not know them all by name either. But that face—now, she would never forget it.

Robin . . . Father . . . surely no such thing had happened to him?

It was not a thought that could be spoken.

After a moment of silence, Beau whispered, "Dove is an angel pony." No fake Frankish accent right now. "She could stamp, snort, neigh to the others . . ."

Rowan nodded. A single sound from Dove would have betrayed them, but the pony had stood as silent as the fog.

And the same cloudy gray color. Each day Beau rubbed more charcoal and ashes onto the pony.

Beau told Rowan, "Your face is all smeared with soot. And bleeding."

"Really?" Rowan lifted her hands to feel for the blood, but stopped herself; her hands, also, were black with soot from clutching at Dove. Trying to clean them, she rubbed them against her own hair, pushing it back from her forehead.

"Now your hair is black."

"So much the better." Rowan gave matters a moment's thought, then said, "Beau, could you get me Etty's cloak?"

"*Mais certainement.*" The Frankish foolery was back. "Instantly."

Strapped behind Dove's saddle like a blanket, the cloak was ample and deep-hooded, worthy of a princess. Thick, warm, water-shedding gray wool. Meant for foul weather. Etty used it only to sleep under. But when Beau had unfastened it from the saddlebags, Ro put it on. She slipped her bow and her quiver of arrows off her shoulders, laid them in her lap instead and covered herself head to toe with the cloak, pulling the hood forward until it almost covered her face, and she saw the forest through a tunnel of shadow.

"So the twigs don't blind me," she explained.

"*Mon foi,* you look like the death specter on a ghost horse, fit to frighten children."

For once Rowan found herself not amused by Beau's babble. "Don't talk like that," she flared.

"*Sacre bleu,* I just joking."

"Well, don't. Don't joke about me and death."

Eight

In days to follow, Rowan continued to wear the cloak, which did indeed protect her face and eyes against the forest fingers relentlessly jabbing at her.

The travelers proceeded in the same careful way they had begun. Beau walked beside the pony. Rook scouted ahead to the northwest; Etty scouted ahead to the northeast. Lionel ranged even farther ahead, hunting.

But danger, when it came, beset Rowan from behind.

When least expected. Dove ambled along a deer trail atop a ridge, her head bobbing and her ears at a placid angle. And Rowan rocked along with the pony's soft walk, her face safe within the cloak's hood, her head down, starting to nod, almost asleep—

Far to the south she heard a feral cry, something between a growl and a howl. A wolf? Or Tykell? Ro's head snapped up, and so did Dove's; Rowan felt the pony's muscles bunch to leap in fright. Just in time Beau caught Dove by the bridle, as Rowan twisted in the saddle to look.

From the ridge she could see far between the trees, for bushes and thickets were just budding, not yet in leaf. And amid the bare trunks of distant oaks she saw something moving, something massive and black.

Turning toward her.

A huge black warhorse that seemed to have two heads.

Ro went rigid. "Lady help us," she whispered. She knew that monster, her mortal enemy, a bounty hunter who rode in armor of black horsehide atop his black horse. The one who had half a dozen times tried to kill her, Robin, Lionel.

It appeared that he had seen her already. But perhaps he had not yet seen Beau behind the pony.

Rowan ordered Beau, "Hide!"

"What? I—"

There was no time to explain. Rowan lifted her foot and booted Beau in the chest, sending her sprawling into a patch of bracken. "Stay down!" she hissed. At the same time she swung her other foot, stirrup and all, over the front of the saddle so that she rode sideward, lady-style, and her bow and arrows slid off her lap to land in the bracken with Beau. Rowan turned Dove away from Beau and urged the pony forward, off the deer trail, down the slope. But not too fast. She did not want to appear to be fleeing. With one hand on the reins she held Dove to a rapid walk. With the other she rubbed ashes from Dove's mane onto her own face and hair, just in case they were not sufficiently smeared already. Then she felt for her dagger, drawing it from its sheath at her belt, keeping it hidden under her cloak.

Scarcely a furlong from where she had left Beau, she heard the hoofbeats of the warhorse closing in at a ramping trot from behind her.

She turned Dove to face her enemy as he rode up to her on his black steed. To face him, and also to place him with his back toward where Beau lay not too well hidden. If he had ridden past the bracken a few paces closer or slower, he would have seen the girl huddled there.

He yanked his steed to a halt with a burly hand gloved in black. All armored in black leather he rode, in the hide of a black horse, and what had been the skin of the horse's head—forelock, ears, mane and all—served as his helm, hiding his face. Glaring through the narrow openings where the dead horse's eyes had been, he towered over Rowan. His war steed towered over Dove.

"Sir Guy of Gisborn." From within the concealment of her cloak's hood, Rowan greeted him in a high, wispy voice as much unlike her own as she could manage. "Well met."

He barked, "You know me, damsel?"

"All who dread outlaws know Sir Guy of Gisborn." Although he was a common, mercenary bounty hunter, she flattered him by titling him a knight. "Look, riding this lonely forest way, I tremble in fear." Indeed Rowan's hand shook on Dove's reins, and her voice wavered most pathetically.

But he did not soften his voice. "Who are you? Let me see you."

Twice before, Rowan had faced Guy of Gisborn, but that had been two years ago, when she had been a skinny short-haired boy-Rowan, chin up, eyes defiant. Once since, Guy of Gisborn had seen her as a girl lying captured and unconscious at the edge of two kingsmen's camp—but it had been nighttime then, and she hoped the firelight had not shown her clearly. And that also had been a goodly time ago. She had grown since, and not just bosoms, as Etty had teased.

Reaching up to pull back the hood of her cloak, Rowan kept her eyes downcast, her chin tucked to her collarbone, and she puffed her cheeks just enough to change the shape of her face, to make her look babyish and stupid. She drew back the cowl to the blackened front of her hair for barely a moment, acting the part of a timid damsel, careful not to look at Guy of Gisborn.

During that moment there was terrible silence. Far away in the hush Rowan heard a pattering sound, soft at first, then drawing nearer like myriad tiny swarming dooms. Rain coming.

She tugged the cowl forward again and hunched her shoulders to make herself small, cowering.

Guy of Gisborn asked, "Why are there ashes on your face?"

Rowan breathed out. He had not recognized her.

"I go in penance," she said, keeping her voice high, wispy and tremulous, "all by myself in ashes and penance to beg my husband, my lord, my master to take me back."

"So you're a runaway bride." Not the least bit surprised that such a young girl might be married, Guy of Gisborn now sounded more insolent than harsh. With foaming mouth his war steed fought against the curb bit, but Guy of Gisborn held the horse still, lolling in the saddle. "Do you know anything of another one, a wench named Ettarde, on a white pony?"

Rowan felt Dove trembling beneath her, poised to

run for fear of the great black steed. She felt her own hand, the one hidden beneath her cloak, clench her dagger hilt. Stroking Dove's shoulder with her other hand, trying to calm the pony, Rowan shook her hooded head.

"Blast and damn, how many girls on ponies wander this wilderness? I trailed you all this way, thinking you were her."

"Good Sir Guy," Rowan appealed to change the subject, "have you seen aught of outlaws?"

"Only the common sort. Naught of that villain Robin Hood."

Rowan felt the first large raindrops of the shower strike her cloak. She saw one land on Dove's shoulder.

Plop.

And there shone a bright white spot, cleaned of ashes, on Dove's hide.

Lady help me!

Hastily Rowan stroked Dove's mane over the spot, but the raindrops kept coming down, harder.

"Days spent to no avail," Guy of Gisborn was complaining, sounding a bit like Lionel.

Indeed. And would he think the same when he saw the gray pony turn into a white one?

"And now it's raining," he grumbled.

"Yes. I must seek shelter." Rowan pulled the reins, and Dove backed away, as eager as Ro to begone.

But Guy of Gisborn slackened rein, allowing his steed to follow her. "We both seek shelter, and safety from outlaws," he declared. "I will ride with you."

Nine

Rowan felt her mind freeze like a partridge hiding in a thicket. How was she to get away? Already the rain had turned Dove's neck dapple gray.

Far off in the forest she saw something else gray. A shadow. A movement.

But even at that distance she recognized that fleeting form: Tykell. It had indeed been Tykell who had sounded that wolfish cry of warning.

And now Ty had ventured nearer.

Behind Guy of Gisborn.

Just in time.

Staring past her enemy, Rowan opened her eyes wide, gasped, and shrieked like a dying rabbit, screaming as loud as she could.

As she had hoped, Guy of Gisborn swung his horse around to look for danger.

Instantly Rowan wheeled Dove in the opposite direction, up the slope of the ridge, and kicked. More than ready to run, Dove lunged into a gallop.

Never before had Ro ridden Dove faster than a jog trot, let alone sidesaddle. There was no time to swing her leg back over the saddle so that she could grip with her knees. Crouching over Dove's neck, head down, ducking branches, Rowan let go of the reins to grasp the pony's mane, hanging on.

Behind her she heard Guy of Gisborn roaring. "What ails you, wench? Outlaws? Wolves? A wolf!" It sounded as if he had caught sight of Tykell, and perhaps set off in pursuit. The noise of his shouting faded behind Rowan.

But she did not dare stop. Guy of Gisborn had tracked Dove before. If he wanted to, he would track her again.

Allowed to choose her own direction, Dove sped along the deer trail atop the ridge. It had been possible, if not easy, for Rowan to keep her seat when the pony was going uphill, for the saddle's high cantle braced her. But now, bouncing somewhere between cantle and pommel, she lost her one functional stirrup, and willy-nilly she dropped her dagger so that she could hang on to Dove's mane with both hands. Every time Dove gathered and leapt, galloping, Rowan felt more air intrude between her and the saddle.

Following the contours of the top of the ridge, the deer trail started downhill. Dove galloped headlong, gathering speed as her hooves slid on the rain-slicked slope. Lurching to one side of Dove's neck, Rowan felt herself part company with the pony, and she curled up like a hedgehog, clutching the cloak around her.

"Ooof!"

Landing on her back, she rolled off the path. Dizzily through the pouring rain she caught a glimpse of a rather streaky, partly white pony galloping away. And then she found herself tumbling like a gray stone down a bumpy slope.

"Oooff!"

This time Rowan hit against some very hard obstacle that halted her about halfway down the hill. The hood of Etty's cloak had twisted around her head and covered her face. Rowan couldn't see. But she made herself lie still as if she were indeed a stone. With her head down, waiting, she listened.

She heard only her own heart pounding, her own breathing and the drumming of the rain.

Cautiously she lifted her head, pushed her hood back and looked around.

She lay against a boulder in the pouring rain. Her body ached from the impact. Why couldn't it have been a bilberry bush or a tangle of grapevine that she had rolled into? The forest hated her.

Trying not to groan aloud, she lay thinking. If Guy of Gisborn had set off in pursuit of Tykell, hoping to kill the supposed wolf for bounty, then all might yet be well. Ro had no worries for Ty, who could run through the forest faster than any horse. And she had no worries for Rook, or Etty, or Lionel, none of whom should be anywhere nearby.

But what about Beau? Galloping after Tykell, Gisborn might have ridden right over Beau's hiding place. . . . A cold serpent of fear rippled down Rowan's spine, and she could lie still no longer. As quietly as possible she clambered to her feet, pausing to look and listen for danger—but all she heard was rain, and all she saw was wet wilderness. Silently she turned back toward where she had left Beau, slipping through the forest step by step, quiet, alert, like a deer.

At first. But within moments her legs ached so much that she began to stumble.

"Toads," Rowan muttered. "Toads take my stupid legs. No. Toads take all man traps." Especially the one that had broken both her legs. She had no staff to lean on. Instead, she clung to the trees. Reaching up, hanging on to low boughs, she hauled her faltering body onward. Rain drenched her upraised arms and face. Her wet hands slipped, and she fell.

"*Filthy* toads!"

Sitting on the sodden loam, remembering how she used to be able to run and hunt from one end of Sherwood Forest to the other, Rowan felt hot tears trying to burn their way out of her eyes. But tears would do Beau no good. Blinking, Ro staggered to her feet again, looked all around, listened, then took a deep breath and trilled like a wren. Although no real wren would ever sing so blithely in the rain.

Then she stumbled on.

But within a few minutes she heard a considerable brush-rattling commotion approaching her at some speed. Guy of Gisborn again? And she, Rowan, outlaw, on foot, with no weapon, not even her dagger?

Lady help me.

But then Ro sighed, blinked and smiled as she saw Beau burst out of a thicket, running toward her.

Like a small black-haired spirit of stormwind, Beau flew downslope, scattering twigs, deadwood, stones and assorted gear. Dropping everything she carried, she whirled into Rowan and embraced her.

Rowan returned the hug, her face against Beau's sopping wet hair. "Sorry," she murmured.

"Sorry? What for?" No Frankish pose now. Emotional, Beau could not suppress her own true accent, that of a Wanderer. "You save my life!"

"I fell off Dove and she ran away."

"So, we find her. Good sense, to get far from that black-horse man. *Brrrr!*" Beau shivered eloquently.

Rowan slipped the cloak off herself and wrapped it around the other girl.

"I not cold!"

"You will be. You're drenched to the skin." The rain was slackening, finally, and the cloak had kept Rowan mostly dry, for good thick wool repels water. Besides, she saw her bow and her sheaf of arrows lying where Beau had dropped them, and she badly wanted them back on her shoulders. Limping to them, she bent over—

"Wuff!"

As wet as the rain but far warmer, a large tongue engulfed her face.

"Tykell!" Dropping to her knees, Rowan hugged the wolf-dog around the thick ruff of his neck. Her chilled hands found the dry, warm fur next to his skin. "Ty."

"You're all right, then," came a gruff voice from behind her.

"Rook!" Letting go of Tykell, Rowan struggled to her feet, turning to face the dark-eyed boy. "Where's—"

"Right here." Etty's voice, and there she was, scooting down the wet slope on her heels. "Who screamed? What happened?"

"The Gisborn Guy!" Beau, who had heard every word that had passed between the bounty hunter and the wispy-voiced runaway bride in the gray cloak, told the tale. Eagerly. In detail. With Frankish flourishes.

". . . then the black-horse man, he ride back the way he come, saying things not nice. La, he cross-eyed with the bad humors. Almost over the top of me he ride where I hide in the bracken, but he not see me."

Gathering up her bow and arrows from the ground where Beau had dropped them, Rowan ran her hands over them—yew bow with ram's-horn tips, flint-tipped elf-bolts in their leather quiver—the gifts of the aelfe seemed to have once more survived intact. Slinging the weapons of an outlaw over her shoulders again, Rowan started limping upslope.

Running after her, Etty called, "Rowan, where are you going?"

"I dropped my dagger."

"Where?"

"When I grabbed Dove's mane."

"But *where?*"

Rowan could not see what more explanation was necessary: She meant to return to the deer trail atop the ridge, locate Dove's hoofprints, then backtrack, searching for the dagger.

Rook understood. "Sit down," he told Rowan. "I'll find it."

"I go find Dove," said Beau.

This made sense in one way, for the pony was more likely to let Beau approach her than anyone else. But it lacked sense in another way, for there was danger in the forest, and while Beau had a bow, she had not yet mastered it; her arrows missed more often than they hit, so how was she to defend herself? Etty declared, "No, I'll go."

Beau's black eyes flashed. *My pony.* "I go."

It was a serious matter, that of the missing pony, and not only because Beau loved Dove. Loose in Sherwood Forest with saddle and bridle, Dove could be taken by any stray peasant or outlaw or thief who could catch her. Or, even worse, her reins might catch on a tree, any part of her harness might become tangled so that she could not move, and she might starve if she were not found.

"We'll both go," Etty offered.

"And leave Rowan alone?"

"For the love of toads," Rowan said, "I can be left alone."

Rook told her, "Sit down."

"Wait. Sit on this." Beau twirled the cloak off her shoulders and tossed it to Rowan. "I go find Dove."

Etty said, "No, Beau, listen. You—"

"I go now."

"I'll go with you."

"No, stay with Rowan!" Voices were heightening.

"We're back where we started," said Rowan, still standing, holding the heavy, wet cloak, her legs aching.

Rook said, "Rowan, sit *down*. Etty, Beau, you stay with her. I'll go for Dove."

"You crazy?" Beau cried. "You go search the dagger."

Rowan said, "I can find my own nitwit dagger." With Tykell at her side, she started limping off again. Stumbling, she put a hand on Ty's back for support.

Three voices cried after her.

"Rowan!"

"Rowan, wait!"

"Rowan, you—"

"What's going on?" called a fourth, plaintive voice. Rowan turned. They all turned.

There stood Lionel, all seven feet of him, blinking and bewildered, leading Dove like a big dog at his side.

With nightfall, the rain started again. A hemlock grove provided shelter of a sort, but with no dry wood to be found, the Rowan Hood band lit no fire. Huddled with the others, soaking wet, Rowan shivered. Yet this night her heart felt warm. Her belly ached, empty, for there had been nothing but greens to eat, but for tonight her heart felt full.

"Dove," Lionel was telling the pony, "despite appearances, this grass is my supper, not yours."

"It isn't grass," Etty told him. "It's cresses."

"Dove," said Lionel, and even in the dark Rowan knew his eyes had gone owlish round, "as you can't graze, you are supposed to browse on the hemlock boughs. By morning I may be doing likewise."

"*Sacre bleu,* that I like to see," said Beau amid muffled laughter. "Lionel, he browse twice as high as Dove."

They joked in defiance of hunger, cold, rain. The way they always did when things got hard, Lady bless them. As they went on with their laughing talk, Rowan grew aware of a small silver embrace on the third finger of her left hand. Although she could no longer feel the presence of spirits in earth and trees and sweetwater, still, she could feel the presence of the remaining two strands of Celandine's ring.

Six rings in one, finely wrought to fit together like a puzzle, Mother's gimmal ring had survived the deadly cottage fire unharmed. A thing of aelfin power, that ring, and the aelfe had spoken through Rowan the day she had made that silver band of many strands the emblem of her outlaw band.

Now Etty wore one on her finger, Beau one on hers. Lionel and Rook wore their strands suspended on thongs around their necks, under their jerkins, so that the rings nestled over their hearts.

Tonight Rowan felt like the weakest strand of the band, almost broken. Not that she had ever called herself their leader or thought of herself as anything more than their comrade, despite the way they seemed to turn to her. But now she felt herself far less than ever before. No aelfin power in her anymore. Worse. Weakness. She was a burden to her friends.

Yet here they remained with her, just as the silver circlet remained intact, embracing her finger. Like a larger embrace, her comrades encircled her. Far more than the strands of the ring bound them all together. And it was this thought that made Rowan's heart feel warm and full even while the rain pelted down.

With her right hand, Rowan caressed the two strands of silver, slipping them up to her knuckle and back again, hugging them with her fingertips.

One of the silver strands remained on Rowan's hand for herself. And one of them waited for someone yet to receive, someone so far unknown.

Ten

By the time birch and willow had come into leaf, two weeks later, Rowan and the others had reached the northern fringes of Sherwood Forest. Rowan rode a booted pony now; Beau had tied pieces of uncured deerskin around Dove's feet to blur their hoofprints so that Guy of Gisborn, or other enemies, might not easily follow the trail. And the booted pony was brown; Beau had stained Dove with juice boiled from alder twigs.

Then, only partly joking, Beau had attempted to eat the cooked wood. She was hungry. All of them were. Meat does not fill a body as bread or fruit would, and sometimes there was not even meat, for hunting while on the move is no simple matter, and at times not even a rabbit blundered into bowshot. As for foraging, this was the worst time of year. Sometimes supper was only wild onions or the eggs of nesting songbirds. Even fish was hard to come by, for fishing requires staying in one place for a time, and they had to keep moving on. Luckily, one day Rook had spied a mess of eels swarming up a brook to spawn, and scooped them out of the water with his bare hands. Poached eel for supper had seemed a feast, although Lionel grumbled that an eel was just a snake with fins.

All of this, they endured for me, Rowan thought as she halted Dove to look at what lay ahead. *My friends. Hungry on my account.* Because she sought vengeance for her mother's death. Otherwise they might still be sheltering warm and dry in Robin Hood's great hollow oak tree.

So it was with a humble heart that Rowan scanned the open, heathery uplands before her. From the concealment of one of the scattered copses at the northernmost reaches of Sherwood, she could just barely see Barnesdale Forest, a low lavender smudge on the far horizon beyond the heather moors. To get to Barnesdale, they must journey across that rolling upland, gleaming golden in the canted light of a sinking sun, its beauty deceitful. The moors offered no hiding for outlaws; Rowan knew that there would be danger. As surely as night was on the way right now, peril would be on the way tomorrow.

And then, beyond Barnesdale, they must journey across open pastureland again before they reached Celandine's Wood. More peril.

For her own sake, Rowan did not care. But what right did she have to endanger all of them?

As if guessing her thoughts, Etty said, "We could try crossing by night, I suppose. Follow the stars."

"And blunder straight into some peasant's farmyard," Rowan said, although her deeper fear was for Dove. What if the pony put a hoof into some unseen rabbit hole, broke her leg?

Etty nodded with her usual serenity. "Well, we've made it this far without starving or being captured."

"Or stepping in a man trap," Lionel added.

"Or eating the snakes or toads," Beau put in, "and because our noses are fastened on our faces not upside down, we no drown in the rain either, la?"

While the others muffled their laughter with their hands, Rowan tried to smile, but could not. Yes, they had come this far alive—but also without seeing or hearing anything of Robin Hood.

Eyes on the lavender line of forest on the far horizon, Ro said slowly, "I wish I knew where my father was."

Etty said, "Wherever he is, likely he's wishing the same of you."

"That's just it." Rowan turned in the saddle to face her friend. "He'll go to the rowan grove, find it abandoned—"

"Probably he already has," Etty said.

"—and he'll be worried, thinking maybe I'm captured, searching for me—"

"Probably he already is," Etty said.

"But he would never dream I'd go so far . . ." Rowan let the thought trail away, but she knew Robin would expect to find her in or around Sherwood Forest.

As usual, it was Rook who asked the hard question. "Do you want to turn back?"

And Rowan saw how the question raised hopeful heads all around her. Even Tykell, sitting on his own bushy tail, looked to her for an answer. But she did not answer, for her heart felt hollow and she did not know what to do.

Looking over her shoulder toward Sherwood's familiar shelter, she scanned the woodland around her.

Violets bloomed now, a carpet of velvety blossoms and heart-shaped leaves between the trees. Rowan wondered whether violets were good to eat.

Or fern fiddleheads. Many of them thrust up between sparse, slender trees. There were no mighty oaks and elms in this grove, only smaller, slimmer maples and poplars and lindens.

Nearby in the copse grew a rowan.

This was to be expected, for rowan trees, far smaller than oaks, grew commonly near the edges of oak forest, where sunlight could reach them. But this rowan seemed not to be thriving. On some of its branches, buds promised foliage and flowers and fruit during the season ahead. But many of its limbs jutted dry, gaunt and the color of ashes, lifeless.

Rowan looked to her own hands, gaunt and pale on Dove's reins.

She studied the rowan tree again. Half alive. Half dead.

The way she felt.

And feeling that way—incomplete, despairing—had already made her remember that other time, two years ago, when she had felt hollow at heart, desperate because she had needed to know about her father.

What she had done then was what she should do now.

But now, as then, the thought made her shake with fear.

Nevertheless, trembling, she slipped down off of Dove. "Leave me here for the night," she told Rook, Etty and the others. "Come back for me in the morning." She handed the pony's reins to Beau. "Take Dove with you."

"What?" On Rook's face Rowan saw a look she scarcely recognized there: surprise.

"Leave me here and come back for me in the morning," Rowan repeated, trying to sound calm and patient even though she was not. Not patient. And far from calm.

"But *why?*" Etty begged.

"So that I can know what to do. So that I can answer you."

Beau gawked, for once speechless. Lionel exclaimed, "We can't just leave you alone!"

"Why not?"

"Because you can barely walk! And anything, anybody could—"

With a gesture of her thin hands Rowan hushed him. "No harm will come to me."

"At least let Tykell—"

"No." Rowan ordered the wolf-dog, "Ty, you go too. Go hunting, catch yourself a fat rabbit."

Lionel persisted, "Keep him here! How—"

"I will come to no harm, I tell you! My kinfolk will be with me."

"Toads," Rowan whispered to herself after the others had gone away, "if my kindred will not hurt me, then why am I quaking?"

Because the personages whom she intended to summon were fey, that was why. They were what the countyfolk called "wyrd": human in appearance yet not human, ghostly yet not ghosts. Spiritous, yet something more than woodland spirits. Folk called them "the denizens," for few dared to speak of them by name: the aelfe, timeless and immortal dwellers in the hollow hills of Sherwood Forest.

Although Rowan would always hold the aelfe in awe—as would anyone with good sense—she had thought she was over her fear of them. Of their otherness.

Apparently not. Her knees weakening, Rowan sank down to sit on the ground under the rowan tree.

Even though she could no longer sense the spirits of trees and earth, wind and water, Rowan did not doubt that she could speak with the aelfe. Any clodpole could perceive the denizens when those ancient, powerful beings chose to manifest themselves. Rowan remembered more than one time when strong warriors had run away screaming from a glimpse of their faces—

Better not to think of that. Better to think, as was true, that the fey blood of the aelfe ran in her own veins. Her mother's mother had been aelfin, driven out when she had married a mortal. In their child, Rowan's mother, mortal warmth had melted the silver moonlight essence of the aelfe into a golden glow.

Mother. Remembering Celandine, a flower of a woman always dressed in green, Rowan felt her shaking stop, felt peace fill her with warmth like a candle flame from within. While mother was alive, Rowan—then named Rosemary—had been unable to learn a wood-wife's simplest spells, but that had made no difference to Celandine. Mother had loved her with all her heart until the day she—

Until the day the lord's henchmen had killed her.

Ro found herself quivering again, this time with rage. *Guy Longhead. Jasper of the Sinister Hand. Hurst Orricson and his brother Holt.*

They would pay.

They *would* pay. Rowan's mind was made up. All she wanted of the aelfe was news of her father, so that she could go on her northward quest with peace of mind.

"My kinsmen," she demanded of the woodland, "I need to speak with you."

All that happened was that the sun sank beneath the horizon, twilight settled on the copse like a gray shroud and a cold wind blew. Shadows and wind might or might not have been a response. Rowan had no way of knowing. She knew nothing anymore except with her mind.

"My kinsmen," she addressed the forest more courteously, "I would like to ask you a question."

Still the chill wind tore at her jerkin. Colder, rougher, harsher.

Rowan remembered how it had been that first time—and the only time, until now—that she had dared to summon the aelfe. She had felt their response like the wilderness-sized presence of a mother turning, half annoyed, half loving, toward a whining child.

But now, in this northern copse, she felt nothing of love.

And of annoyance . . . more than mere annoyance.

She remembered the first time she had caught sight of those wilderness denizens: the night the magic of Lionel's singing had drawn them to encircle his campfire, faint humanlike figures aglow and afloat between the trees. Perhaps if she called Lionel back here to this copse and asked him to play his harp—

No.

No, this was a family matter. Between her and them, her kinsfolk whom she barely knew. Only twice had she ever spoken with them, and they had answered her in riddles.

"My kinsmen?" Rowan requested one more time of the darkening forest. "Would you please bespeak me? I have need of your wisdom."

Nothing happened except that twilight darkened and the chill wind still seethed.

Rowan's lips narrowed to a thin line. "Well," she muttered, "it would seem that I need to make a fire."

Stiff, she hoisted herself to her feet and began to break the dead branches from the rowan tree.

A mystic tree, the rowan, growing sometimes like the mistletoe on the shoulders of the oaks. Rowan wood gave protection against lightning. Diviners used branches of rowan to find precious metal. And dried rowan was an ardent wood, good for need-fire.

Good for the propitiation of spirits.

When she had broken from the rowan all the deadwood she could find, Ro laid it down and, in the last ghostly light of the day, went looking for oak trees. Need-fire must always be started in the hollow of an oak log.

Finding oaks a bit farther back toward Sherwood was easy, but finding a thickness of dead oak Rowan could handle was harder. By the time she dragged in a section of a rotting branch, night was falling and so was she: staggering, her aching legs ready to give way under her.

Sitting down on the damp ground, with her dagger Rowan split the oak branch lengthwise. Laying one of the sections like a trough of pulpwood before her, she whispered, "By your leave, spirits of fire," picked up two dry sticks from the rowan tree and began to rub them against each other.

Need-fire could not be kindled with embers or from flint and steel. Need-fire had to be made the old, old way. Ro knew what she had to do, but not how much pain it would cost her. Never before in her life had she attempted need-fire.

Somewhere in the night frogs spoke, fell silent, spoke again. A few stars shone through a veil of cloud. Half dark and dead, like the rowan tree, the moon gave only dim light.

Rowan could barely see the rowan sticks she rubbed together, but she could feel her arms begin to ache. She set her teeth and rubbed dry deadwood harder, faster, without stopping, until her arms felt half crippled with pain, the way her legs did when she walked. Still she did not stop. She must not, even though tears burned in her eyes. This was the meaning of need-fire. The measure of Ro's effort and suffering was the measure of her need. She forced herself to keep rubbing the sticks together faster, harder, with no way of knowing how much longer till something besides tears burned. In the darkness she could not see smoke.

The pain in her arms turned to agony, then passed beyond agony into numbness. As if another part of her had died. But about that time Ro smelled something hot.

Sudden small flame blazed up from the rowan twigs.

Tears ran down Rowan's face as she let her tortured

arms at last be still. Looking at the fire, she saw it through the water in her eyes. Flames like russet waves. Paradox of life, Etty would have said.

Shakily, barely able to control her movements, Rowan laid the flaming sticks in the pulpy hollow of her oak log.

From everywhere and from nowhere, as if emanating from earth itself, a bodiless voice spoke: "What do you want of us, daughter of Celandine?"

Eleven

A voice neither young nor old, neither male nor female. Nor, indeed, human. The aelfe spoke.

Ro found herself trembling again as she placed more dry sticks on her small fire. She had to force herself to look up from the flames.

Just at the reaches of the firelight, dim silver human-sized mists swirled up between the trees.

Rowan swallowed hard, firmed her jaw and made herself scan the—faces, yes, moonglow faces of kings and warriors and matriarchs and maidens, ageless young-old faces so beautiful, Rowan ached with longing to reach out for them, yet so eerie that she could scarcely bear to look upon them.

Nevertheless, look she did, because once before, on that other occasion when she had summoned the aelfe, they had manifested themselves to her as Robin Hood, spirit of Sherwood Forest.

But not this time. Father was not here, not even in spirit.

A stinging feeling in her eyes, perhaps from the smoke of her need-fire, made Rowan look down as the aelfe spoke again. "What do you want, daughter of Celandine?" Cold, impatient, the voice came from none of them and all of them.

Rowan found herself unable to bespeak what she wanted. Instead, she whispered, "You are angry with me."

The voice sounded merely indifferent now. "Was your mother ever angry with you?"

"Of course. But—you have turned away from me." Or so she felt, with her face torn by the twiggy fingers of the forest, her body sore from its stony bones.

"Does the falconer turn away from the falcon?"

Trust the aelfe to speak in riddles. Rowan tried again. "Every step of my way here, you have opposed me."

"As the darkness opposes the light, or as the light opposes the darkness?"

Rowan clenched her teeth in frustration. There was no getting sense out of—

"Go back."

Ro's mouth dropped open, and she blinked. Never before had the aelfe spoken to her so plainly, and for that reason she could not understand them. She whispered, "What?"

"Go back to your rowan grove." The voice deepened, darkened. "You stray this way for no good reason."

Ro stiffened. "But my reason could not be better!" Anger flared in her, hot and sudden, like need-fire. "I have sworn vengeance. And now I know the names of those who slew my mother."

"They slew her? How so? Only you can kill her truly."

More nonsense. More riddles.

"Go back to where you belong," they told her, "Rowan Hood of the Rowan Wood."

Rowan hardened her jaw, lifted her head, shook it. "And do what? Sit there and let my comrades care for me?"

"Use the gifts your mother gave you, daughter of Celandine."

They had told her this before, more than once, but she had never fully understood. Even less now. Whatever gifts of aelfin power she had possessed, they were gone. She said, "I cannot go back. There is nothing for me to go back to. I must go forward."

"So you think."

"So I know. I ask you only this, wise ones: Where is my father?"

"Where he belongs."

That could mean anything. "Is he alive? Is he well?"

"You cannot tell? Use the gifts your mother gave you, little one."

Little one? Rowan stared, unable to tell whether that was mockery she heard in the voice, or tenderness, or—

It mattered not. Before her eyes, the aelfe faded away, leaving her alone with her need-fire and the distant voices of frogs.

"Onward," Rowan told the others in the morning— a fine morning, sunny, with breezes whispering a promise of primroses and cowslips to come, on the meadows they would be crossing.

Etty nodded placidly and handed Ro a slab of cold cooked venison to eat. "We have plenty of meat. A stag walked right into our camp last night. *Beau* shot it."

"*Beau* did?" Beau could barely shoot the tree she stood under.

"*Sacre bleu,* it surprise me too!" Beau flashed her brilliant grin. "Maybe the denizens send the stag, yes?"

Rowan said, "I doubt it."

Lionel asked quietly, "You saw them? You spoke with them?"

"Yes." Still seated by the ashes of her fire, under the struggling rowan tree, Ro gnawed at the food Etty had given her. Her arms, sore from making need-fire, ached so badly, she could barely lift the meat to her mouth. Nevertheless, she tore at it with her teeth. When had she last eaten? As she swallowed, her stomach began to ache almost worse than her arms.

Lionel prompted, "And?"

"And what?"

"The denizens. What did they say to you?"

"The usual. They vouchsafed me riddles."

"They did not tell you where Robin Hood is?"

"No. But . . ." Rowan hesitated only a moment; she knew she owed her friends the truth. "But they did tell me one thing plainly. They told me to go back to the rowan grove."

No one gasped, but no one spoke either. The silence screamed.

Rowan said, "I will not go back. I cannot. I must go on. But if any of you wish to turn back, you should do so."

Silence lasted just a moment too long before Lionel grumbled, "Don't talk nonsense, Rowan. How would you get where you're going without us?"

"I told you before, I will crawl if I need to. Go back if you judge that is what you should do."

"I'm the one who put this maggot into your mind," said Etty grimly. "I'm coming with you."

"Of course I'm coming," Lionel said. "I'm too big for

anyone to harm me." Not true—they all knew he lived in dread of combat, for if he injured his hands, he might not be able to play his harp anymore. No one smiled.

Beau glanced from Rowan to Dove and back again. "I go with you," she said.

"For Ro's sake or for the pony's?" Etty teased.

"Both!"

"Thank you." Rowan nodded to them, then turned to the one who had remained silent, who usually remained silent. "Rook?"

He said, "I'm going back."

He, the one who respected the aelfe the least, and common sense the most? Those words from Rook took Ro's breath away.

Lionel began to bluster. "Rook, how can you—"

"Let him be." Rowan regained her breath and her voice. "I said if anyone wanted to turn back, they should. Go with my blessing, Rook."

With both hands, softly, slowly, Rook drew from under his jerkin the thong from which hung his strand of the gimmal ring. The silver circlet swung in the air, glinting, until he cradled it in the palm of one hand.

Was he—did he mean to take it off? Was he leaving the Rowan Hood band? Forever?

Rowan's heart squeezed. Please, Lady, no, this was all her fault. This could not be happening.

Rook looked at Rowan, a long, level gaze. Then he turned to Beau, to Etty, and finally to Lionel. He said, "I swore my loyalty to all of you on this."

And without another word he placed the silver ring back into his jerkin, over his heart.

Then he turned, and empty-handed—Rook never carried a bow and arrows, or even so much as a quarterstaff—with no weapon but the knife at his belt, he walked away. Southward.

Quickly. Rook moved like hawk shadow in the woods. In a moment he was gone from view.

Silently the remaining four prepared to venture northward onto the open moors. Trying not to look like outlaws, Beau and Etty wore the archil tunics over their kirtles. All of them lashed their bows and arrows onto Dove's baggage behind the saddle. As befit a horseback rider, Rowan wore Etty's helm, trying to imagine she looked like a squire even though Etty's cloak covered the rest of her. Once Lionel had set Rowan in the saddle, he helped her arrange the cloak to conceal the outlaw weapons behind her saddle as well. Then, being a minstrel despite having no bright-colored clothing, he took his harp out of its bag and carried it in his hand.

From atop Dove's back Rowan looked at all of them: a wolf-dog who followed her when he cared to, and the

friends who followed her because they had so chosen—
Etty, Beau, Lionel.

But not Rook.

Lady be with Rook.

Ready? her glance questioned the three who remained. They nodded.

Nudging her heels against Dove's side, Rowan rode out into the open. Lionel strode past her to lead the way. Beau walked beside Rowan on one side, Etty on the other.

None of them looked back.

The sky felt like a great blue eye watching them, Rowan thought, as they traversed the windy brow of the first rise, the next, the third. They passed plovers shrieking and trembling on their nests amid the heather. They passed bony, spotted cows grazing on the new furze while the cowherd, a boy almost as rawboned as the cattle, gawked at them. From distance to distance they passed cottages built of turf and thatch. A man yoking his oxen stared at the travelers as they walked by. A gaunt old woman watched them from a cottage doorway as a dirty child clung to her skirt. A goose girl peered at them from a meadow, and her geese, great gray snake-necked birds, opened their snapping bills to bark like dogs.

Growling, Tykell turned toward the geese.

"Ty," Rowan commanded. "Let them alone."

But as if he were deaf, the wolf-dog stalked toward the barking birds; he killed rabbits, he killed squirrels, he killed partridge—why should he not kill a goose?

"Tykell!" Rowan hated to speak to him so sharply, but it was necessary. "Let them alone! Do you hear me?"

Ty stopped where he was, but he would not look at her. Overhead a magpie flew, laughing, a bird of ill luck.

"Onward," said Rowan wearily.

As the day wore on, they saw many a magpie fly. But they also saw meadowlarks soaring and heard them sing. The spring air blew sweet with the fragrance of wildflowers: cowslips, bluebells, a promise of butter-cups and wild roses to come. And celandine—but no, Rowan thought, celandine would never froth and flow and quiver on the meadows as commonly as cowslip; celandine, like the silver valley lily, was a woodsy flower. And although the very brightest of starflowers, celandine was shy, blooming sparsely in secluded dells.

There was beauty under these open skies, but Rowan found it a shiversome beauty, too naked.

Toward sundown Lionel bartered with a cottage wife, trading venison for hen's eggs and barley cakes. The band of travelers chose a hollow in which to camp, and there they sat and ate the best meal they'd tasted in many a day. But it was as if a ghost sat with them. They did not speak.

At twilight Tykell gave Rowan a look over his thickly furred shoulder as if to ask, "By your leave?" Because he had not come over to her to have his head patted and his ears rubbed, she knew he was annoyed with her. Sighing, she told him, "Go ahead; go hunting." Geese should be safe in their pens now, chickens in their coops, sheep in their cotes. The wolf-dog slipped away to wander the night.

Still the others sat without saying a word.

Until full dark had fallen. Then a voice spoke. "I hope Rook has something to eat."

Rowan blinked, realizing it was Beau. She was not used to hearing Beau speak so simply and without foolishness.

"A pox on Rook! The traitor," Lionel complained so fiercely that Rowan knew he shielded pain with the hard words.

Etty said, "Lionel, please don't be more of a nitwit than necessary. Rook—"

"Is a traitor and a fool." Yet Lionel began strumming his harp, as if to comfort himself.

Rowan said quietly, "We know Rook is no fool."

"Then how can he believe himself to be still loyal to the band?"

They fell silent again, for they did not know the answer to that question. In this too-open place, darkness seemed to press in from all sides, held back only by firelight and the soft notes of Lionel's harp.

In the morning, when they awoke, Tykell had not returned.

Rowan had long since learned that she had to trust the wolf-dog to go about his own business as he saw fit, and find her when he wanted to. But this time, Rowan sensed, it might be a long while before she saw Tykell again, if ever. In her heavy heart she knew that the wolf-dog, like Rook, had turned back to Sherwood Forest.

"Surely we will encounter him along the way somewhere," Lionel said as they made ready to travel.

Rowan answered only, "I hope so." She did not speak her more true thought: that Lionel had said the same about Robin Hood.

Twelve

"Toads take everything," Rowan said. "I was just starting to hope we might reach it by nightfall." She pointed toward Barnesdale Forest, no longer a low lavender blur on the horizon, but now a blue-brown mass not too far ahead.

However, between Rowan's band and Barnesdale Forest ran a river that cut through the moorlands like a knife. A river swift, deep, steep of bank.

Halted on a hillside, they studied the gray water. This was a gray day altogether. Sky the color of Rowan's borrowed cloak cast darker shadows on the hillsides. And in the river ran water a colder gray, the color of steel, but swelling like a warrior's muscles.

"No more than a stone's throw wide, but fit to drown us just the same," Lionel said. Having once spent some unintentional moments in just such a river, he knew the power of water running wild during the springtime rains.

Etty asked, "Have you crossed this torrent before, Rowan?"

Two years ago, Etty meant, when Rowan had fled through these same lands on her way southward to Sherwood Forest.

"I must have." Ro frowned, thinking. "But it's hard to remember those days." Bad days, desperate, starving, grieving days just after her mother's death.

Mother. Dead.

At the thought, her heart burned with the sting of the names branded there.

Guy Longhead. Jasper of the Sinister Hand. Hurst Orricson. Holt, also Orricson, brother of Hurst.

The others were watching her.

"I think it gets shallower somewhere," she mumbled. Blurrily she seemed to recall wading across, wet to the waist.

"La, see, the fleur-de-lis," said Beau, pointing at spears of green thrusting up from the river's verge, not yet in bloom.

"Ding-dong Belle, it's called iris flower," Lionel grumbled. "What—"

"You no call me Belle! No ding-dong. Sot-head, fleur-de-lis means shallows upstream. Maybe a crossing."

"She's right," Etty said. "The irises grow in shallow water, and then the bulbs get washed downstream."

They turned upstream, with the river to their left, keeping their distance from its muddy verge.

The gray sky darkened, threatening yet more rain.

"There," Lionel said, pointing ahead with one hand, "a ford."

A place where the banks of the river lowered, and the river widened and ran more shallow, and folk waded across, fording the river for want of a bridge. A cart path ran down to the ford, disappeared into the water and reappeared on the opposite side, by a copse of poplars.

Up until now Rowan and the others had stayed away from trodden ways, where too many eyes might see them. And where they were more likely to meet with brigands, or some lord's men-at-arms, or bounty hunters, dangers of all sorts.

Rowan scanned the cart track as far as she could trace its path northward, on the far side of the river, and southward. "No one in sight," she murmured.

"*Mon foi,* then let us, how Euripides say, seize the moment?"

"*Carpe diem,*" Etty murmured. "Seize the *day.* And I don't think it was Euripides. It was . . ."

"It doesn't matter," Lionel grumped. "Let's *go.*"

They headed at a fast walk down the hill toward the path and the ford. Rowan started to gather up the gray cloak to keep it from trailing in the water. Riding Dove, she would get her feet wet, nothing worse, but the others would be soaked to their chests, chilled, on a day with no sun to warm and dry them afterward. They were likely to take ill with the coughing sickness, and it could kill them as readily as an enemy's sword.

"Somebody get up here with me," Rowan offered as the path turned to mud. "Beau, climb on." Her thoughts ran as swift as the river. "Etty, you wait here, Beau can leave me on the other side and bring the pony back for—"

These plans remained incomplete.

"Halt!" bellowed a man's deep voice. "Stop where you are, or die." Out of the poplar grove on the far side leapt a great gray warhorse carrying an armored knight, his lance upright at his side, his broadsword flashing, the visor of his helm down to hide his face. His steed's next galloping stride sent it into the river, splashing toward Rowan and her band across the ford. So huge was the horse that the water barely reached its belly, but sprayed higher than Rowan's head.

They stopped where they were, indeed, for terror froze them. They stood like wood.

But then the burning heart of anger in Rowan flared

forth in words. "Halt yourself, brute!" she screamed like a hawk at the knight bearing down on her.

The knight yanked on the reins. His charger plunged to a stop in midstream. His lance, pointing skyward in its holder by his stirrup, swayed like a pine tree in a storm. "You're no squire!" he roared. "You speak with a damsel's voice. Why do you wear a helm?"

"Because I so choose." Seldom had Rowan spoken so fiercely.

Lowering his sword, the knight actually sketched a sort of bow at her from his saddle. "I beg your pardon, damsel, for my mistake. I thought you a squire, and I have taken a vow to challenge any man of warrior blood who seeks to cross this ford."

Ettarde spoke up. "You bear no pennon upon your lance." Even though she stood ankle-deep in mud, she sounded imperious. "No plume to your helm, and no device." Instead of showing an emblem, the knight's shield gleamed entirely black. "What is your name and who is your lord?"

In the middle of the rushing river, his gray warhorse surged like a spirit of the gray water, while he controlled it with one hand on the reins. Swinging the steed toward Ettarde, he retorted, "I have also taken a vow to reveal my name and allegiance to no one."

Vow? Nonsense. Rowan started to tremble, more fearful now than fierce, but she kept her voice hard. "Then you're a brigand." Plainly this was a robber knight, taking what he would from travelers who had to use this ford—the only way across the river.

"Nay, I rob no one. I take only a fair toll from those who pass this way."

Toll? Fair? To whom?

"And," added the knight with the black shield, "it is for the sake of honor that I engage them in combat."

Honor? He might like to call it that, as he liked to call thievery a toll, but plainly he spoke in threat. Still, Rowan kept her voice edgy and flat, like a dagger. "Very well. For what price may we cross?"

"What have you to offer?"

"Little enough."

"Why, then, I fancy some fun with you. Yon varlet shall cross swords with me. You." The knight raised one gauntleted hand to point at Lionel. "Prepare to fight."

"Me?" yelped Lionel. "But I'm a minstrel!" He held his harp in front of him as if it could shield him.

"No common minstrel grows so tall. You are warrior thewed, and I will battle you. Provide yourself with a weapon." The knight sent his charger at a splashing trot toward them.

"I have no sword!" Lionel cried.

"You shall have one of mine." Parlous great hulking

clodpole, he wore a spare sword at his right side; Rowan saw it slapping his leg as he approached.

Lionel tried again. "But I have no horse!"

"I shall dismount to fight you. And you may have my shield, if you like."

"How very generous of you!" Lionel sounded ready to laugh, cry or scream. Tall and strong he might be, but he stood small chance against this bulky oaf all armored like a beetle in breastplate and greaves and chain mail clanking from his helm down over his gray woolen tunic to his knees.

"Lionel," Rowan ordered, "run! Go back, join Rook."

"I can't just leave you!"

"We're all going." Already Dove, shying, had leapt away sideward. Rowan turned the pony to flee—

She gasped. Necessarily she halted Dove, for her path of retreat was blocked.

"*Sacre bleu!*" Beau exclaimed. "Another one!"

Down the hillside toward them strode a great bay warhorse bearing a knight much like the first, except that instead of flourishing his sword, he couched his lance. Spurs clashing, he urged his steed into a ramping trot. His armor clanged, his chain mail rang like war bells. He bore a large white shield blazoned with a black X. One of Marcus's knights? But if he recognized Etty . . .

He seemed not to. "Out of my way, churls," he

snapped at Rowan and the others from behind his lowered visor.

"Gladly!" Lionel spoke for all of them as they scrambled aside from the path and away from the river.

The newcomer knight roared to the first, "Ho, you at the ford, knight with two swords!" He made a mocking jingle of it. "I have heard of your renown, and I have come to knock you down. Couch your lance!"

Doing so, the other one replied, "Prepare to die."

Thirteen

At first Rowan thought she would not mind watching.

These were knights, after all. Like the knights on horseback who had invaded her mother's forest, set fire to her mother's cottage. Henchmen of a heartless lord, or brigands with no loyalty but to themselves, let them battle all they liked.

From a safe distance up the hillside—although truly, no distance seemed safe—unable to cross the river while the combatants held the ford and the path, Rowan and the others saw the warhorses thunder toward each other. Each knight aimed the steel tip of his lance at the other's helm, and each aimed true; with a hundred times hammer force, steel struck steel.

But the helms withstood the blows, the lances glanced off and the knights reeled but kept their seats.

They swung their steeds around and charged each other once again along the bank of the river, lances aimed at breastplates this time. Both struck so hard that the lances splintered. And the shock of impact hurled both knights to the ground.

The war steeds ran away, but not far. Stepping upon their own reins, they stopped, snorted, then lowered their massive heads to crop the grass. To those chargers the combat was a matter of indifference now, over.

But not to the knights. Staggering to their feet, they drew their broadswords.

"Beware!" bellowed one.

" 'Ware *yourself,* hound!" roared the other. Then the swords clanged.

To Rowan, those metal-clad battling figures seemed barely human, such strange creatures smiting at each other for such unaccountable reasons. More like trolls, if there were such a thing as trolls, with their great hacking swords swinging. Or like lions fighting, if there were really such a thing as lions. Or dragons—

But then she saw puddles of red on the mud at the riverside, and she knew that blood came from men, not dragons, and she had to press one hand to her mouth to keep from crying out.

She heard Lionel ask Etty, "Is the one with the white shield a knight of Lord Marcus?"

"I do not think so." Ettarde's voice sounded as taut as a bowstring. "I think one of my uncle's knights lies dead, and this one has borne away his shield."

Although Rowan had known they might really fight to the death, something in Etty's tone made her close her eyes.

But it was even worse to hear the clangor, the shouts, the thudding impact of blows, without knowing what was happening.

"Lady help us all, neither one of them will yield." Lionel's voice shook.

There sounded a battle roar that twisted into a scream of agony. Rowan's eyes snapped open. She saw the knight with the black shield striking right through the other's larger shield and into his head. Blood like a red plume ran down from the challenger's helm, yet he did not fall, but swung at the other one so fiercely that he cleaved his shield as well, and his sword bit into the defender's arm.

Rowan turned her face away. Beneath her she felt something shaking, and did not realize it was Dove; she thought the very earth quaked.

She heard Lionel whisper, "They're in the water." Then, "They're both down! They'll both drown!"

Rowan could not help it; she looked. For a long moment, she saw only two shattered shields drifting down the gray river.

But then, like monsters coiling out of chaos and darkness, both knights surged up to stand staggering under the great weight of their own armor, swaying against the pressure of the current. Their combat had carried them into midstream, where the water ran fierce and swift up to their chests.

Both at the same time lifted their swords, hacking at each other. Rowan saw the river water turning red. Biting her lip, lowering her eyes, she saw that Beau stood with her arms around Dove's neck, hiding her face in Dove's mane. Etty had grabbed hold of Lionel as if he were a tree to support her. When Rowan looked up again, both knights had somehow staggered back to the shore of the river where they had begun, blundering up the muddy bank, barely able to stand.

"Is it over?" Rowan whispered.

Lionel shook his head. "I doubt it."

And even as he spoke, one of the knights—Rowan could no longer tell which was which—one of the water-soaked, bloodstained, mud-caked warriors, with a great effort, struck the other with his sword.

The other one heaved up his own heavy weapon and struck back.

Rowan could not bear it anymore. "Stop it!" she screamed, shoving Beau aside with one hand as she kicked Dove into a wild downhill canter.

Behind her, the others cried out.

"Rowan, no!"

"Are you insane?"

"Wait! You'll get yourself killed!"

Rowan paid no heed. But as she reached the battling warriors, Dove snorted at the scent of blood, shied away from the red pools, whirled to a stiff-legged halt and would approach no nearer.

One knight had beaten the other to his knees, but he himself staggered backward and fell down. The kneeling one slumped over, barely holding himself out of the mud with his elbows. Rowan saw the sheath at his right side. It was the knight with two swords, the one who had held the ford.

He called hoarsely, "Who are you, Sir Knight? Never before have I met a fighter who could match me."

The reply came faintly. "I am Holt, son of Orric, Lord of Borea."

Rowan felt a strange cold storm of emotion blow through her, leaving her chilled to the bone.

The other one gave a terrible cry. "My brother!" And he fell down, unconscious.

Cold and hollow to her heart's heart, Rowan barely noticed as Lionel ran up beside her to seize Dove's reins.

Crying out in his turn, Holt Orricson floundered to his hands and knees, crawling through the mud to the other. Jerking at the man's half-destroyed helm, he got it off.

Etty and Beau stood by now also, staring at the fainting knight. A savage, bearded face, but bloody, bruised and still.

"No! Oh, Hurst, no!" The other one tore off his own helm and flung it into the river. Stunned, Rowan stared at his face, much like his brother's, but with tears cleaving runnels in the blood and dirt.

Hurst Orricson's eyes flinched and opened, looking up at Holt. He moved his bloodied mouth soundlessly, then spoke. "We're cursed," he said faintly. "You have killed me, my brother, and I have killed you."

Lionel placed the bodies of Hurst and Holt, warriors and murderers, side by side on the hilltop. Then he and Beau and Ettarde raised a cairn of stones over the corpses, to keep the carrion birds from pecking out their eyes. It was long, hard, somber work. Rowan labored with the others until her legs would no longer support her, then sat on the heather, whispering the blessing of the Lady over the dead. By the time stones covered the bodies, the sun was setting, casting a red glow on the end of the day as Lionel marked the place with the knights' two swords, their bloodstained blades plunged into the earth.

Rowan and the others spent the night in Hurst's pavilion, on the other side of the river within the poplar grove, all of them silent and subdued despite the great wealth they found under its canvas roof: gold and jewels, but more to their purpose, food, drink, salves, blankets, clothing—all manner of luxury, including soap.

Traveling onward rather late the next day, freshly washed in the river, Rowan and her companions had horses to ride, and plenty to eat: the knights' saddlebags carried dried apples, bread, cheese and smoked pork. Ro, Beau and Etty each wore one of Hurst's flowing tunics draped and girded to serve as a gown. Even Lionel had found among the loose-fitting garments a bright yellow jerkin only a little too small for him, sky blue leggings and a rose-red hat and sash. Decked in his favorite colors, with mismatched colorful trappings on his gray steed, he appeared every inch the carefree traveling minstrel.

But he had little to say. None of them did. Rowan rode silently behind Etty on the other warhorse, the bay, and Beau just as silently rode Dove, across open, windy moorland where plovers cried.

Finally, around midafternoon, Lionel turned his head to ask Rowan, "Why did you try to help them?"

He spoke gently enough, but Rowan clenched her teeth, for she considered that it had been weakness, mollycoddle folly, that had made her forget her vow of vengeance, jump off of Dove, kneel in the mud by the two dying knights and try to bind their wounds.

Yet Lionel did not sound as if he were teasing.

She gave him a hard look. "Why do you ask?"

"I have my reasons." Reining in his horse to ride closer to her, Lionel asked again, "Why did you?"

Rowan sighed and turned her eyes forward. "I don't know. Stupidity." Hurst Orricson and his brother Holt had died within moments of her arrival. Even if they had not already lost so much blood, they would have died. Each of them bore more than one fatal wound.

As if in cahoots with Lionel, Etty asked, "Would you have saved their lives if you could have?"

From her seat behind the saddle, Rowan could not see Etty's face. But Etty did not sound as if she were teasing either.

Still, Rowan gave no answer. She did not know the answer.

"La, Rowan, I think it is because of what Petrarch

say." This from Beau, riding Dove at a trot to keep up with the larger horses. She had removed the deerskin wrappings from Dove's hooves, for what was the purpose? A blind tracker could have followed the hoofprints they were leaving now.

Etty raised her brows. "Petrarch?"

"He say, 'What the brain forget, yet the heart remember.' "

"I don't recall that in Petrarch."

Rowan burst out, "I think it is because I have the brain of a mudhen."

"Think you so?" asked Lionel owlishly.

"Yes. I am a lackwit nincompoop to be doing a favor for my enemies."

"Indeed."

"Yes. But it doesn't matter. We would have needed to go to Borea regardless."

"We *would?*"

"Yes."

"Why?"

"To find the other two."

Jasper of the Sinister Hand. Guy Longhead.

Knights of Lord Orric of Borea.

Two years ago, fleeing to Sherwood Forest, Rowan had done so in part to escape becoming a peasant in Lord Orric's village or a wench in his fortress.

Hard old Orric of Borea was perhaps the last man on earth whom she would wish to visit.

Yet by some unaccountable perversity of the Lady, Hurst Orricson, dying in Rowan's arms, had begged her, "Warrior damsel, prithee, tell our father where we lie." And looking upon his beaten face, she had thought, *This is one of them, one of those who set his torch to the thatch and killed my mother*—but the thought had seemed meaningless at that moment, as death rattled in his throat and he had whispered, "Promise me." Willy-nilly she had nodded. Unshed tears stinging her eyes, unable to speak for pity, she had watched her enemy die.

As her other enemy lay already dead.

It was as if the Lady had blessed Ro's quest for vengeance with the deaths of those two plus the great good fortune of food, clothing and captured horses. Yet in no way could Rowan put the name of blessing to the cold and tangled winds blowing in her heart, the frigid battle raging there.

Fourteen

H orses travel far *fast*," Rowan whispered in awe as
they halted at the northern edge of Barnesdale Forest.
Spring had advanced only a little; elms put forth pale
green shoots now, and sticky chestnut buds hinted at
clusters of leaf to come. Only a few days had passed,
and Rowan did not feel ready to be where she was: sitting in a tall steed's saddle, looking across Lord Orric's
demesne. Before her lay pastureland, then freshly
plowed land where beets and barley would grow, then
a huddle of huts, and then, towering over the village
that surrounded it, the walls of the lord's stronghold.

And beyond the stronghold, more strips of cropland
where peasants ploughed with oxen, and more waste-
land where boys herded sheep and goats, and in the
blue distance, a soft mound almost like a low-growing
violet-colored flower.

"See yonder forest?" Rowan pointed it out to the others, trying without quite succeeding to keep her voice from faltering. "That's Celandine's Wood."

Her home.

"*Would* that we were going there," said Lionel.

"We are."

"If we live."

Etty ordered, "Lionel, hush. Seven feet tall and you whine more than the rest of us put together."

"Because I know what's ahead! No wind blows more fickle than a lord. If we just stroll into Orric's hall and tell him—"

Rowan said, "We won't."

All eyes turned to her eagerly. Beau exclaimed, "*Mon foi*, you have changed your mind?"

"No. I must keep my promise. But there is more than one way to beard a lord."

She explained her plan.

It took only a few minutes to get down off the horses and prepare. Everything that marked them as outlaws—bows, arrows, even belts or shoes made of deerskin—had to be hidden out of sight. Etty still had the cowhide boots she had worn from Celydon, and Lionel wore a pair he had taken from one of the dead knights, but Beau and Rowan slipped off their boots and went barefoot. Weapons, supplies, all clothing of Lincoln green and brown, Etty's cloak, everything they wished to keep in their possession they wrapped in blankets and strapped onto Dove. The pony's mane and tail had grown unkempt, and her brown dye had come off in patches, making her skewbald; to anyone who did not study her aristocratic head and neck, she looked like a humble pack animal. Leading Dove by a makeshift rope put together of reins and harness, Beau got up on the gray steed behind Lionel. Rowan and Etty shared the bay steed, but this time with Rowan in front, at the reins, for she knew the way.

All four of them looked at one another and found no words to say.

Then they rode out of Barnesdale Forest and across the grazing lands toward Borea.

Strangers did not often come to this far northern place. Never had Rowan felt so many eyes upon her, upon all of them, as when they rode up to the edge of the village. Men shouted to one another, ploughman to smithy to miller to carpenter; women with spindles dangling from their hands gawked from the doorways of the wattle-and-daub huts; chickens squawked and scuttled, dogs barked, half-naked dirty children jostled either to get away or get closer. Some of these people perhaps had met with Rowan before, when she had been Rosemary, the woodwife's daughter. But she pushed aside fear that they would recognize her, for they had seen her seldom. Moreover, she sensed how much the years since her mother's death had changed her.

Rowan felt the great warhorse beneath her starting to snort and champ the bit, arching its neck, showing off, the vain overgrown donkey. "Toads squat in your ears, horse," she muttered. Her fists tightened and sweated on the charger's reins as she led her comrades around the edge of Borea village toward the track that would take them to the fortress.

There. A dirt road that cleaved the village and ran across earthworks, Lord Orric's failed attempt at a moat, to the gate. Once she had found the way, Rowan wrestled her horse to a brief halt and beckoned Lionel to take the lead.

Ro's horse went along more quietly now, following the gray, and her grip on the reins relaxed. Although her eyes looked straight forward at the lord's stone and timber walls, she found herself mindful of Celandine's Wood also, a not-too-distant peaceful presence behind her back.

And something else behind her back as well. A stir, a murmur, footsteps. She turned her head.

Beau, looking around also, confirmed what Rowan glimpsed. "La, half the village, they follow us to see what passes!"

"Who goes there?" shouted a man's voice from the fortress.

Rowan's head snapped around. Let the village folk gaggle like geese if they liked.

"Halt!" shouted the same voice. "Name yourselves and your business!"

A guard. The gates stood open, for it was daytime, and folk bustled in and out: washerwomen, scullery girls, a peasant leading a donkey half buried under sacks of seed for planting. But the guards still watched to challenge strangers.

Three of them, in helms and quilted tabards, barred the way to the gate with pikes at the ready. A fourth stood atop the guardhouse; it was he who had shouted the challenge.

Rowan and Etty halted at the rear of the small caval-cade. It was Lionel, in the fore, who spoke. "We are travelers bearing dire news for your lord." The band had agreed that it should be Lionel who dealt with the guards while the rest of them hung their heads and tried to look maidenly.

"Travelers? Of what nature?"

"I am a minstrel." As before, Lionel carried his harp in the crook of one arm. "These are my sisters who accompany me."

Someone snickered. "Indeed," said the chief of

guards with a sneer in the word. "Your sisters. And how do you, a minstrel, come by such various sisters and such fine horses?"

Taking no offense, Lionel replied quietly to the second question only. "The pony is mine. The two warhorses we have brought here to return to your lord. One of them belonged to Lord Orric's son Hurst. The other, to his son Holt."

A gasp and a muttering went up from the crowd of villagers behind them, and for a moment the chief of guards' mouth fell open. Then he demanded, "You bear news of young my lords Hurst and Holt?"

"I do."

"Enter."

Hearing the command, the three guards with pikes lowered their weapons and stood aside. But Lionel and his entourage made no move toward the gate.

"Nay," Lionel told the chief guard, "we'll proceed no farther." He vaulted down off his gray steed to stand, a humbler visitor, on the ground. "I respect the lord's grief, and also I fear his wrath, should I tell him that his sons lie dead."

A gasp and a clamor went up all around, such a hullabaloo that the chief guard shouted to be heard. "Dead! How? By whose hand?"

"They slew each other."

"What!"

"They wore visored helms. They bore captured shields, rode captured horses. They did not know each other as they fought. And . . . and they both prevailed."

The villagers' clamor had risen to wails, screams, cries not so much of grief as of fear. "It's the curse!" some peasant woman keened. "The house of Orric is accursed forever for murdering the woodwife!"

The shrill words pierced Rowan like an arrow between her ribs, taking her breath away. She tried to turn, to demand of the woman what she meant, but Etty, sitting behind her in the saddle, gripped her with both arms. The strength of that hug warned Rowan not to give herself away.

But Beau, perched atop the gray, turned to the villagers. "What is this?" she cried with just the right thrill of shock, just the right height of curiosity. "A curse?"

A dozen eager, frightened voices vied to tell her about it.

"They slew the woodwife, and her curse—"

" 'Woods witch,' the lord's men called her."

"The more fools they. She was a wise woman, a healer, but they—"

"Her daughter, too, a good child, wishing harm to no one. Yet the four knights rode against—"

"They never meant to kill the woman and the girl, only frighten them."

"And for what reason? Because—"

"To drive them out."

"You simpleton, it was for the sake of power, nothing more. No good—"

"They set the thatch afire. And instead of fleeing, the woodwife—"

". . . nothing right since. A murrain sickened the cattle—"

". . . lay down and cursed the house of Orric and died."

"—winter so cold half the old people and infant babes perished—"

"Jasper of the Sinister Hand took to drink and—"

"—and then summer so hot and dry the wheat shriveled, the wells failed—"

"Lord Orric's men marched against Celydon and only half of them came back."

"—and beat his wife so cruel, he slew his unborn child, and when he saw what he had done—"

"Guy Longhead is a lost soul entirely."

"And now young lord Hurst and young lord Holt—"

"—ran away half naked. They say he's starving out there in Celandine's—"

"Hush! Don't say her name. You'll bring her dying curse down on all of us."

All this Rowan heard with her back turned, her shoulders hunched iron hard, her eyes on what was happening among the guards. Go tell his lordship, the captain had ordered them one after another, and each in turn had refused.

"How dare you disobey me to my face!" the man atop the gate was roaring now.

One of the guards replied flatly, "I'd rather beard you than his lordship."

"You know the penalty! You'll be flogged!"

"I'd rather be flogged then dead."

Rowan dropped the reins, pulled herself free of Etty's arms, swung one leg over the horse's neck and slid to the ground. Her stiff legs panged like heartache as she landed, but she kept her feet. Wobbling, barefoot, she limped forward to stand before the gates. "I'll go," she told the captain of guards.

A gasp rose all around, not least from Beau and Etty and Lionel, for the whole plan had been to keep themselves away from Lord Orric; Rowan's passion for revenge had never included him, for he had seemed beyond her reach.

Lionel cried, "Are you mad? Ro—"

Her glance stopped him just in time from saying her name. "Even Lord Orric would not smite a girl," she told him. And, she might as well have said, a cripple. "I'll go."

Lionel said, "I'll come with you, then."

"No. All of you stay here. And until I return, tell no one where lie the bodies of Hurst and Holt." This knowledge might be a way to ensure her safety, should she need to do so.

She gazed at each of her comrades in turn, willing them to understand why the plan had changed, why she must do this thing. Lionel returned her gaze with sheerest horror, and Beau with bewilderment, but in Etty's eyes she saw understanding. Not approval, but acceptance. Etty had taken hold of the bay horse's reins.

Rowan turned to one of the guards and told him as if she had a right to command, "Show me the way to his lordship. I will tell him of the fate that has befallen his sons."

Fifteen

Even as Rowan hobbled across the courtyard between the walls and the lord's central stronghold, the
tower called the "keep," maids and men-at-waiting came
running out. And page boys and scullions and even the
men-at-arms, fleeing, for alarm spreads as swift as a falcon's flight among servants. As Rowan's guide led her
up the stairs to the keep, they met a flood of frightened
folk pouring down.

Within, a deep voice roared, "What has chanced?
Stand and speak, cowardly dogs!"

The guard who was leading Rowan stopped and
beckoned her to pass him. "I'll go no farther," he whispered.

She nodded to him and walked onward, step by
painful step, entering the dim stone-and-timber passageway within.

A few laggard servants scattered past her with wild cries, like quail in flight. Only Rowan faced Lord Orric, striding toward her in the torchlight with his beard jutting, his fierce face much like those of his sons. He had been holding court, it would seem by the crimson velvet that arrayed his tall, powerful body, but there was nothing velvety about the naked sword he bore in his hand.

Rowan looked him in his fearsome face and said in a voice like milk, "I have come to tell you what has happened to your sons."

He halted, standing almost within arm's reach, and glared at her. She stared back. She felt the stone cold, cold under her bare feet, but not much else. The chill wind that had been blowing through her heart had seemingly emptied it. This was the lord who had hated her mother, but Rowan felt too weary to hate him. Nor did she fear him. He could brandish his great sword with all his might and she did not tremble. She felt barely alive, so she did not care whether she died.

He barked at her, "Who are you?"

"A stranger who has seen a strange, sad thing." Her white voice scarcely seemed her own. "I will tell you what I have seen with mine own two eyes. No more, and no less."

She folded to the floor of the passageway, for her suffering legs would not bear her weight much longer. And as he stood over her, glowering, she told him the story almost as if it were a fairy tale. How two knights had met at a ford, the gray knight who challenged all comers and would not reveal his name, and the other knight who had heard of his renown and come to cross swords with him. How mightily they had battled, each unhorsing the other, each striking the other with mortal wounds. How at the last, as they lay dying, the one had asked the other's name, and had cried out, "My brother!" How they, Hurst and Holt, had embraced and died.

And how she had promised to bear the news to their father.

As she spoke, she never moved her gaze from Lord Orric's fierce bearded face, his yellow mouth set in a snarl. And his scowl never changed. But without even clouding, his eyes rained. Tears showered down his craggy cheeks and watered his thorny beard.

And when she had finished and looked down, she saw that his sword hand had sagged to his side. The broadsword's double-edged blade lay against his velvet-clad leg, pointing toward the ground.

Silence, except for, winging in from a distance, the sweet notes of a harp, the honeyed tones of a tenor voice. Out by the gate, Lionel was playing and singing a favorite ballad:

"In hidden glades of wild Sherwood
There lives an outlaw fair and free,
An outlaw bold as gold, yet good
Of heart. Folk call him Robin Hood . . ."

From the distance, Rowan would not have been able
to make out the words or the tune if it were not that she
already knew them so well. She felt the music comfort
and strengthen her even as the thought of her father
made her heart ache.

Lionel sang on:

". . . with his maiden daughter, brave and good,
an archer with a healer's hand
on which there shines a mystic band,
Rowan Hood of the rowan wood."

Rowan's heart panged harder. Why must Lionel sing
this song here, now, at such a time?

Perhaps in an attempt to charm or soothe the lord?
But Orric seemed not to hear the minstrel at all. He
stood silent and his hard, wet eyes looked faraway, as if
searching for his dead sons. "Hurst and Holt dead by
each other's swords," he said heavily at last. "This is far
more than mere mischance. This is the work of the
woods witch's curse."

Rowan shook her head. Still speaking with the same milky calm, she told him, "My mother never put a curse on anyone."

The lord's narrow eyes seemed to spark like flint. His breath hissed inward between his clenched teeth and his sword swept up as he leapt back. Crouching, weapon raised and stabbing at air, he glared as if Rowan were a viper coiled upon his floor, ready to strike him.

Rowan did not move, did not flinch, did not lift her arms to shield herself. "My mother was a healer who wished all good and no harm to anyone." Not even her voice rose. "If she were here, the touch of her hands would ease your pain." A power that had once belonged to Rowan herself, and to her own muted surprise she found herself wishing she still had that power so that she could lay her hands upon the fierce lord's head to assuage his grief. Odd, she thought, too weary of her own emotions to call herself a mollycoddle for pitying this man. Odd, because he was the one—except for those who had actually set torches to the thatch of Celandine's cottage—Lord Orric was the one whom she should hate the most.

With her voice still milk in a cup of candor, she asked, "Why did you send them to kill her?"

"I did not!" The denial burst out of him even though he still crouched to strike. "I told them only to drive her away." Lord Orric stepped toward Rowan, looming with lifted sword. "Why did she not flee from them?" he roared at Rowan as if it were all her fault.

"She could not. She was at one with the cottage and the glade." It was hopeless, Rowan knew, to try to explain the wonder that had been Celandine to this hard-fisted lord. Hopeless to explain to him the goodness or the rootedness of her mother's woodsy magic. Impossible to make him see how Celandine had been the breeze in the trees of Celandine's Wood, the fire on the hearth of Celandine's cottage, the sweetwater in Celandine's spring, and could not have lived elsewhere.

Rowan explained it to him another way, also true. "She spent all her power in sending a spell of protection upon me."

"Aye, and a spell of vengeance to curse my sons for spite. And poor Jasper, out there in the wilderness, running mad. And Guy, gone evil."

Rowan looked him in the face. "I tell you, my mother cursed no one."

His wet eyes widened storm wild, his hands shook beneath the heavy sword, the sword quivered as if it would leap upon her of its own accord. The lord's whole body quaked with rage. He screamed, "No curse, you say? And what do you call it, then, that has sent you, her daughter, here to tell me—"

"You think my mother cursed *me*?" Rowan shot back. "To have me witness such bloody dealings, such bloody death? And then to have me come here and face you in your wrath? To send me in here as you see me, powerless, weak and lame, a beggar wearing a dead man's shirt? Whom shall I say has cursed *me*, my lord?"

Glaring at her, he could not speak, only cried out like a bear impaled on the huntsman's spear.

"Do you wish to slay me, my lord?" she inquired, gazing up at him, unblinking, blank, a suckling babe.

He gulped, gasped, panted for breath, then stood back and lowered his sword. "Get you hence," he ordered, his voice as rough and ragged as oak bark. "Quickly."

Rowan struggled to her feet. "I am sorry, my lord," she said. But as she turned and pattered away from him barefoot over the cold stones, she wondered at herself. Sorry? For Lord Orric? *Weakness,* she reproached herself. *Weakness and folly.* Her only regret should be that she had not yet avenged her mother's death.

"Why?" Lionel demanded as soon as they had left the fortress and village of Borea behind them. "Why did you go in there?"

To defend her mother's honor, Rowan wanted to tell him. But she could not answer. Since the moment she had returned to the others from the lord's fortress, she had been shaking so hard, her teeth chittered. Terrified, now that she was safe, or as safe as an outlaw ever could be. Now that it was over.

Now that, trembling, she was walking with the others, because the distance to Celandine's Wood was not great. And because Dove, nodding along behind Beau and Etty, remained loaded to her ears with baggage.

Scowling down at Rowan, Lionel insisted, "You could have been killed. Why did you do such an insane thing?"

Rowan wondered if indeed she were insane. Right now she was leading the others toward Celandine's Wood, yet she could not remember why she needed to go there.

"Rowan—"

"Lionel, hush," Etty told him, her usually placid tones a bit weary. "When Rowan finds out why, you'll know it."

"But *mon foi*," put in Beau, sounding puzzled, "is it not obvious? For to look on his face as she told him. For revenge."

Oh, Rowan thought. Yes. Revenge. That was why she was limping toward Celandine's Wood, for revenge on the next one, Jasper of the Sinister Hand. Folk said he had sought refuge there.

Yes. That was it.

"Is that it, Rowan?" asked Etty at that exact moment. "Did it do your heart good to see Lord Orric suffer?"

The question was put not ungently, but it struck Rowan like a blow. She flinched, her eyes wincing shut with pain worse than that of her aching legs. Stumbling, she fell to the rocky ground, facedown in the prickly gorse.

Without a word, Lionel picked her up as if she were no more than a child, cradling her in his arms. He strode onward, carrying her quite a bit faster than she had been able to walk on her own.

She should have told him to put her down or she would shave his head with Etty's sword. But she felt as if she had no spirit left, no defiance of her own misery, no pride. Letting her head rest against his chest, closing her eyes, she allowed him to carry her along as if she were a baby.

No one spoke. In the silence Rowan heard the clopping of Dove's hooves on rocks and clay, the singing of meadowlarks high in a rain-washed sky.

It had happened on just such a day as this. . . .

Rowan opened her eyes, turned her head and looked. From her sideward vantage all seemed strange, yet strangely familiar. Carrying her easily, Lionel strode up the very slope where she had once gathered coltsfoot upon that fateful day. Edged with rowans, Celandine's Wood spread like a green flower ahead.

Rowan said, "Put me down."

"In a minute. Once we're in the forest."

"Put me down *now*. I can walk."

"That is debatable."

"Lionel . . ." Two years ago, when he had barely known her, he had obeyed her without even knowing why, because of the force of—something in her. But whatever that power had been, it was now gone.

Toads take everything.

Misery heated into frustration, frustration blazed into anger, anger fired Rowan with strength to struggle in Lionel's arms. "Confound you, Lionel, put me *down!*"

Last time, he had done so. This time, however, he became stubborn. "In a minute! Once we're safe amid the trees."

"*That's* debatable," came Etty's weary voice from behind. "Safety. Anywhere."

"Just the same." Lionel ducked to pass under the low boughs of a rowan at the edge of the woods.

"Put me *down,*" Rowan told him from between clenched teeth.

"In a *minute,* my dear little girl."

Rowan's temper snapped almost audibly, like a twig. With a wordless cat-snarl she flailed, squirmed, reared in Lionel's arms, pounded her small fists against his chest.

She truly wanted to hurt him, but she could not, blast it. She was just too weak, and he was just too much bigger.

But she did succeed in slowing his steps and making him grumble, "Ungrateful wench, hold *still* until the others get here." Halting under the first tall tree, an elm, Lionel swung around to look for Beau, Etty, Dove.

"Let me *go,* I tell you!" Rowan struggled wildly, clawing at Lionel's neck.

"Stop it!" Annoyed, he tightened his grip on her.

From somewhere close at hand in the forest shadows, a man's fierce voice shouted, "Unhand her, lout! Or I will kill you!"

Sixteen

Rowan landed on her hind end in the forest loam as, utterly startled, Lionel dropped her. Looking up from her sudden seat on the ground, she saw him whip out his dagger, crouching and turning, peering this way and that in search of the unknown enemy.

Struggling to her feet, Rowan snatched for her own dagger, the only weapon she wore because, toads take it, all the bows and arrows and swords remained packed and hidden on Dove. The plan had been to leave the things out of sight until mantled in the safety of Celandine's Wood.

Safety?

Beau and Etty stood just within the shelter of the trees, frozen, staring. Dagger in hand, Rowan staggered two steps toward Dove, toward her bow and arrows, but then she stiffened and stared as well.

At something pale and uncanny.

Out of the shadows of elm, ash and maple sprang a scrawny, bony, nearly naked man—capering. Like a child playing horsie, he galloped on his own two bare feet toward Lionel, flailing at the air with a broadsword that looked as if it had been used to chop firewood. Pulling on imaginary reins, he drew his horse of air to a halt with his left—hand? No, just the stump of his wrist. Perhaps he imagined a hand there, as he seemed to be imagining reins and steed.

His was the unlined face of a young man, yet hair as white as bone sprouted wildly from his head, white hair tangled in elf-knots as thick as a fist, long enough to brush his shoulders. Over a crooked nose that had more than once been broken, his bushy white eyebrows joined so that a single scowling line, chalky against his weathered skin, crossed his forehead. He wore only rags wrapped around his middle.

Woodwouse. Wild man.

Flourishing his battered sword and glowering up at Lionel, facing the much larger youth without any sign of fear—indeed, within arm's reach—the one-handed man ordered, "Go. The woodwife sleeps in her woods, and I stand guard. No one comes here. Get you hence."

Lionel sheathed his dagger, lifting both hands in a

gesture of peace. But he seemed at a loss for words. "I, um," he said, "we, um, we——"

"Go, I tell you!" The wild man crouched as if to strike, his voice louder, more threatening. "No one shall trouble Celandine ever again. Get out!"

Lionel took a step back.

Rowan took a step forward and called, "Jasper."

The wild man's sword wavered, and his eyes turned to her, widening. Then they narrowed and he shook his head. "You are not my wife," he said.

"But you *are* Jasper of the Sinister Hand."

"No more!" It was fey, almost wyrd, the smoothness of this wild man's face, and there was something wrong, fixed and glittering about the look in his eyes. Fiercely, gaily he brandished his left arm with its stump of wrist. "No more bad hand. I cut it off."

Rowan felt both her breath and her heart stop for a moment. In that moment she heard Beau and Etty gasp.

"He's lost his mind," Beau murmured.

Yes, Rowan knew, it was true. The man was crazed. Jasper of the Sinister Hand ran mad.

"Left hand," Etty breathed, standing close behind Rowan. "That's the one he cut off. He is—was—left-handed, that's all. *Dexter* means right, *sinister* means left."

At the same time Jasper declared, "It must never lift sword or torch again. Never."

Rowan knew, but did not care, that the man was mad. It mattered only who he was. Her breath and voice returned in a blaze. "You set fire to the cottage thatch!"

"Four of us did. One at each corner." Again the man looked at her, and this time his face paled, and he staggered, ashen. His heavy sword dropped from his limp hand to the forest loam. He whispered, "You—you are the daughter of Celandine."

"Yes." The word far sharper than the fallen sword. To Rowan's knowledge the man had never seen her before, yet it surprised her not at all that he recognized her. Their meeting felt fated.

"But how does he know her?" Etty cried. "No one in the village—"

Jasper addressed Rowan as if the question had come from her. "Your angry spirit has haunted the grove since the coltsfoot bloomed. Day and night, your vengeful face floating like a shadowed oval moon before my eyes."

"Lady have mercy." Etty's voice had dropped to a whisper.

Lionel murmured, "So that's what happened to her."

Ignoring both of them, Rowan gave Jasper of the

Sinister Hand a curt nod. Turning her head slightly, to those behind her she said, "Somebody get me my bow."

Etty answered in a hard voice, "Get it yourself."

Without fear Rowan turned her back on Jasper to look at Ettarde. The princess met her commanding stare defiantly, without flinching. Rowan looked at Beau, who hunched her shoulders and turned her head away but did not move from the place where she stood.

Lionel remained at guard, towering over the strange wild man, standing between him and the others but laying no hand upon him.

Lips pressed together, Rowan limped past Etty and Beau to Dove—the pony stood browsing on the shoots of young blackthorn. Hanging on to Dove's mane to support herself, Rowan fumbled one-handed at the fastenings that bound the pack. There were many. The task of untying them took time. Somewhere in the branches overhead a wryneck bird sounded its hissing cry, again and again. Minutes passed, yet no one moved or spoke.

At last Rowan found her bow and arrows. She strung the bow, took a single elf-bolt from the sheaf and limped back toward Jasper of the—Jasper of the woods, now. Woodwouse. Hair white with suffering, coiled with insanity. He stood waiting for her.

Lionel broke the silence, his voice hoarse. "Rowan, no. Don't."

"I must. I took a vow—"

"But you can't just kill a man . . ."

"*You* can't," Rowan retorted, for Lionel had refused to hate his murderous father. At the time, she remembered, she had admired his uncanny gentleness. But now she felt nothing but annoyance at his interference. That, and a cold wind blowing in the hollow of her empty heart. And sharp, stubborn anger like a spear point at her back to drive her onward.

The wild man, Jasper, faced her with a wide-eyed, childlike gaze. "You are going to kill me?"

"Mine is the blood right. You killed my mother."

He blinked, then as if he had not understood, he asked again, "You are going to kill me?"

"Yes."

"Good." His eyes glittered, happy. "I am a bad hand. Cut me off."

"No," Lionel begged.

"Yes," said the woodwouse. "I cannot sleep; I hear voices in the moonlight. I cannot eat; I see blood on the grass in the sunshine. I am glad to die, if it is quick. Daughter of Celandine, how will you do it?"

The answer: a single arrow to the heart. But Rowan

found that she could not answer. She could not speak. Some invisible, inexorable fist had taken hold of her throat. Scarcely ten paces away from Jasper she stopped, nocked her arrow, leaned into the arc of her bow and pulled the string back to her ear, taking aim at his naked chest.

This was her moment.

This was her vengeance.

This was her right. The blood right.

And they all knew it. No one moved to stop her.

He—the villain—Jasper could have run away. In her pain, Rowan moved slowly. Almost she offered him a chance to run. But he faced her with his mad mouth open in a smile, his eyes wide open and fixed upon her, sparkling like gemstones. "Quick," he repeated.

No one else spoke. Beau, Etty and Lionel stood mute as stones. Why did they only stare in horror? Why did they not speak? *No, Rowan, don't!* they should have been begging. Why would they not help her defy them?

Every muscle and nerve stretched and taut, Rowan trembled with strain. She found her eyes blurring, burning; she wanted to close them and had to force herself to keep them open. Daughter of Celandine, the villain called her? She did not deserve to be so titled, did not deserve to be called Rowan Hood, daughter of Robin, either. She hated herself, her own weakness.

Coward!

Clenching her teeth, Rowan let the arrow fly.

Seventeen

The bolt sprang from the bow.

Singing an arrow's swift zinging song of death.

But that elf-bolt seemingly trailed a harp string of gold to tear open Rowan's heart. It was not the arrow's song, but Lionel's, that she heard in her mind:

". . . an archer with a healer's hand
on which there shines a mystic band,
Rowan Hood of the rowan wood . . ."

The instant that bolt flew, while her eyes still met her victim's, all the goodness that had ever been Rowan Hood rushed back into her. With her whole body, spirit and soul she remembered what it really meant to be the daughter of Celandine, and she would have given her life to have that arrow back in her hand. She remembered what it really meant to be the daughter of Robin Hood, and the horror of what she had done knifed through her with the worst pain she had ever known.

Dropping her bow, she screamed, "No!"

But the arrow struck.

Jasper fell.

"No!" Sobbing aloud, Rowan ran to him and plunged to her knees beside him, weeping so hard she could barely see, could not tell whether he was alive or dead. Blindly her hands felt at his bare, ribby chest, encountering blood, encountering the shaft of her arrow. Pressing there to stop the bleeding, she choked out between sobs, "Is he—is he dead?"

Without waiting for anyone to speak, she knew: No, he was not dead. Not yet. Under her hands she could feel the rise and fall of his chest as he breathed, could feel the muffled rhythm of his heartbeat.

She had to save him.

But how? She had no aelfin powers anymore, and not even any of the helps such as an ordinary nurse might use, no healing herbs, no—

Water. It was water she needed most. The magical, healing sweetwater of Celandine's spring.

There was no time to be wasted crying. Dashing the tears from her eyes with her fists, Rowan leapt to her feet. "Lionel!" she cried to that large personage close at hand. "Bring him, follow me. Hurry!" She ran.

Like a deer she ran into the woodland where she had spent her childhood. She knew every turning, every tussock, every tree, yet all seemed eerie, strange for being so unchanged. And small. Linden, oak, elm, hazel, and then seemingly after no time at all, she burst into the clearing where the cottage had once stood.

Celandine's glade.

There the grass grew velvety thick and green, as it always had. Greensward covered the hummocky ground where the cottage had stood. That, and something more: lilting long-stemmed yellow flowers clustered everywhere, glowing almost as bright as the sunlight, the golden westering light of late day.

But there was no time to look at flowers. Whirling, Rowan saw that, yes, the others had followed her, with Lionel in the lead, the injured man in his arms.

"Does he yet breathe?" Rowan demanded.

"Yes, indeed." An odd sort of kink choked Lionel's voice.

"Lay him down gently on the grass. Cover him, keep him warm. And somebody bring me water from the spring." Rowan pointed the direction toward where the sweetwater flowed at the far end of Celandine's glade.

"Hurry." She drew her dagger, snatched up the hem of the long tunic she wore and slashed into it in order to use the cloth for bandaging.

But as she tore the first strip of cloth, she realized: Lionel had not laid the hurt man down on the grass. No one had gone for blankets or water. They were all just standing there.

Rowan glanced up to look at Etty, Lionel and Beau. Three in a row, watching her with an expression on their faces that seemed utterly unfitting.

"What are you smiling at?" Rowan yelled.

Etty said, "We're glad to have you back." Tears shone in her eyes—tears of happiness?

"What?" Had they all gone mad? Rowan stamped her foot. "I shot that man. He could die. I need *water* to wash his wound. Go get—"

"Rowan, take a breath." The quirk in Lionel's voice, as if he might either laugh or cry, made her listen to him. "Sir Jasper is all right." Lionel set the white-haired woodwouse down on the ground as Rowan had ordered, but instead of sprawling there in a faint as Rowan expected, the man sat up, alert and silent, looking at her.

Bewildered, Rowan gawked at the wild man.

"Your touch stopped the bleeding," Lionel said. "Your bolt had no more than pricked his shoulder. That was the worst shot I've ever seen you take." Lionel's voice quivered with mirth or emotion. "The arrow fell out on our way here." Holding it in his hand, he offered it to her—Rowan saw the elf-bolt extended toward her, yet seemed not able to move or comprehend or accept.

"You have already healed yon madman," Ettarde told her.

And then an unexpected voice spoke. "In body and in mind," said Jasper, and his was not the voice of a madman at all. "From my heart I thank you, daughter of Celandine."

His eyes, gazing up at her, no longer glittered, but glowed warm with gratitude.

Vehemently Rowan shook her head. "But I tried to kill you! I don't deserve—"

"*Sacre bleu,* Rowan, if we get what we deserve, we all get spanked and put to bed with no supper," Beau interrupted happily. "That is what Plato—"

"There's no such thing in Plato!" Etty complained. "Beau, have you ever read Plato?"

"Me? I no read. I make things up. It work just as good." Not pausing to enjoy the expression on Etty's face, Beau turned back to Rowan. "Ro," she asked, all innocence, "tell me, how your legs feel now?"

Rowan gasped, gawked, then screamed and started to cry, but this time her tears were the warm rain of joy.

She felt arms go around her, and she leapt for gladness, jumping and jumping as everyone hugged her. She broke away and flung herself into a cartwheel across the velvety grass thick with yellow blossoms: celandine flowers. Up into the air whirled her legs, then back down to the ground, well and strong again. As strong as they had been before the man trap had broken them.

Eighteen

W ell," Rowan tried to joke, "as no one has fetched
water from the spring, I suppose I had better go get it
myself."

Really, she needed a few moments alone to embrace
in her mind the wonder of—of everything. Everything
that had happened, and everything that *was,* glowing
in the sunset light, here in her mother's glade. Where
she had left scorched, blackened ground, she now saw
lush grass starred with myriad flowers. Where she had
piled the ruins of the cottage into a cairn to cover her
mother's body, now there grew more soft mantling
green, more sweet flowers: celandine blossoms, Mother's
namesake flower, rayed like daisies but with petals of
glossy yellow, shining bright. Their fragrance filled the
glade, the air, the golden sky. Never had Rowan seen so
many celandine flowers together.

Jasper had said they bloomed there always, even in the winter's snow.

Perhaps Jasper was still crazed?

Or perhaps . . .

Striding away from the others, heading toward the spring with her leathern flask in hand, Rowan considered another possibility, a perchance that swelled her heart with comfort.

"Thank you, Mother," she whispered to the forest glade. "Thank you for everything." For sunshine, for celandine flowers, for the wonder of being able to bound along on two sound legs—the same great goodness that had given her the gift of life itself now gave her these things. Rowan lifted her arms to embrace her mother's presence in the air, and her eyes prickled warm with happiness.

Ahead of her, at the far edge of the glade, she could see the water of Celandine's spring gleaming in its stone-lined hollow beneath a great tree, an oak almost as massive as the one in Robin Hood's dingle. In the canted late-day sun rays, the oak cast a sharp shadow, but the water in the spring caught the light and mirrored it back to the sky. Almost as green as one of Celandine's dresses, that sky, blue overwashed with gold. Almost as green as the grass so soft under Rowan's feet. She thought she had never seen anything so lovely as that sky, that color, that water.

Kneeling at the roots of the oak, Rowan placed her hand into the sweetwater spring tricking down amid ferns into its pool, letting its cool flow caress her fingers for a moment. "With utmost thanks," she murmured, "and by your kind leave, spirit." Then she leaned forward to fill her flask.

The pool tried to warn her.

Mirrored in the water's surface: an enemy form.

Black.

Lunging.

Just as Rowan glimpsed it, before she could move, before she could even shout to alert the others, a burly hand grasped her by her braided hair and yanked her to her feet. Screaming, Rowan twisted and struggled to her utmost, trying to draw her dagger—but she succeeded only in pulling her enemy a few paces into the open before he wrapped a hard grip around her from behind, lifting her nearly off her feet and pinning both of her arms to her sides. With his other hand he held before her eyes a deer-skinning knife. Ro froze, her gaze fixed on that hand gloved in black leather, that foot-long razor-sharp blade.

"You others," the man roared across the clearing,

"not a move out of you, or I'll slit her throat here and now."

With an effort, Rowan shifted her gaze to her friends. Standing amid a mess of gear they had been unloading from Dove, taken as badly off guard as she had been, Lionel and Beau and Ettarde stood helpless. Among them, weak and shaking and white-faced, with a blanket wrapped around his thin shoulders now, Jasper lurched to his bare feet and staggered two steps forward. "Guy Longhead," he cried in a kind of pleading surprise.

"Mad fool, be silent or I will kill you too." Guy's tone dripped contempt.

Rowan felt a searing shock of recognition that burned away her fear for the moment. She spoke calmly. "Guy Longhead," she said, "and Guy of Gisborn, one and the same. I should have known."

The setting sun cast his long shadow on the grass, as black as the horsehide he wore, pricked ears rising from its head like the horns of a demon.

"Rosemary, bastard daughter of the woods witch," he mocked her, "and Rowan, bastard daughter of a thieving outlaw, one and the same. I should have known."

His harsh voice sounded from above and behind her head. She could not see him, but she could imagine the hatred in his eyes behind his black leather visor.

"It took me less than a day to remember where I had seen that face before," he growled. "You'll befool me no more, wench."

And he set the blade of his knife to her throat.

Rowan clenched her teeth. *I will not scream.* She could not help wincing, tucking her chin against the knife, but she forced herself to keep her eyes open and be silent. *He can kill me but he cannot make me beg or scream.*

She drew one last breath—

"Stay your evil hand, Guy of many names," spoke a low voice that made Rowan lift her head, wide-eyed, made her heart pound with awe that supplanted her terror—for that voice came from everywhere and nowhere, from oak tree and elm woods and greengold sundown sky and myriad celandine flowers that would stay open all night, that would never close, not even for winter's snow.

"My kinfolk," she whispered.

And there in the glade they stood as plainly as she had ever seen them, translucent warrior forms advancing upon Guy of Gisborn, fierce men and proud women wearing helms and bearing shields and swords.

Through their silver moonglow bodies Rowan saw Jasper fall to his knees and hide his face. She saw Beau, swaying where she stood, grasp Etty's hand for support. But Lionel, who had met the aelfe before, stood tall, and Rowan knew he felt a surge of hope in his heart.

She knew because she felt such hope herself—for a moment. As the aelfe drew their swords, spectral silver crescent swords that blazed like cold fire—

But then she felt Guy's grip upon her tighten, with no tremor of fear in it.

"Scare-spooks," he growled, "you may have frightened me once, but no longer. What can you do to me with your swords of air? Go away."

And Rowan remembered how, two years ago, Guy of Gisborn had been the one man in Nottingham not ensorcelled by the beauty of Lionel's music. Such mysteries meant nothing to him. The aelfe meant nothing to him.

They did not go away. But they stood where they were, at a small distance from Rowan, and they spoke with a somber, gentle voice. "This is what we feared, Rowan, little one. The other three killers paid on their own for what they had done; such is the way of mortal life. Evil recoils upon the evildoer. There was no need for you to pursue them. But this one—he has paid with his soul, and against him we cannot help you."

Swallowing hard, Rowan felt herself smiling, for she found herself looking into her mother's face. The foremost of the helmed women, Celandine gazed back at Rowan with all the sorrow and love and pride of the world in her fern-green eyes.

Rowan spoke strongly. "Go ahead and slay me, Guy of No Soul. A rowan tree will spring up from the earth upon which my blood falls, and I shall be with my mother again."

And she felt the razor-sharp edge of the knife bite into her throat. She felt a trickle of blood run down her neck. She sensed more than saw Lionel crouch to leap, too late for her, yet he'd risk his own death—

"But wait," Guy growled, and his blade paused where it pressed into the skin of her throat. "It is not just you whom I want. I shall have all you outlaws."

No. No, were friends and comrades to die on her account? Rowan felt her strength turn to water and drain away from her like rain.

As if sensing her despair, Guy of Gisborn raised his triumphant voice. "I shall kill you all, one after another. You, minstrel oaf, if you wish your precious Rowan Hood to live another few moments, throw away your dagger."

Slowly Lionel did so, his face moon white.

"And you others. Throw them over your shoulders."

Etty tossed away her weapon, and so did Beau, neither of them quite able to look at Rowan. But she saw with a pang to her heart that Lionel kept his stricken gaze upon her, a lifetime of unsung songs in his eyes.

Guy of Gisborn commanded, "Now take three steps toward me."

They obeyed.

Gleefully their captor roared, "Now *kneel,* outlaw vermin—"

Thwok.

And even before Rowan heard that meaty sound of impact, before she heard her enemy gasp and felt him let go of her, before she leapt away and spun around to see him topple on his face, even before she saw the gray-fletched arrow jutting from his black-horsehide back— she knew.

She knew, because once again she could sense in the wilderness a beloved presence.

"Father!" she cried. "Oh, Father," as Robin Hood ran out of the woods, dropping his longbow to hug her tight against his chest.

Nineteen

Mother! Mother?"

Stepping back from Robin, Rowan explained, "She was just here," and turned to scan Celandine's glade. But already the aelfe were melting away like mist, dissolving into air. Within an eyeblink they disappeared.

Shakily Jasper rose to his feet.

"Let me get this ugly thing out of here," Lionel grumbled, bending to drag Guy of Gisborn's body into the woods.

Beau and Etty ran to the far end of the clearing to grab Dove's bridle, one on each side, hanging on as Dove burst into a flurry of bucking and kicking. Giving vent to pent-up emotions the equine way, Rowan surmised, but Tykell wasn't helping, dashing out of the woods to nip at the poor pony's heels—

Tykell?

"Ty!" Ro cried.

"Wuff!" At Dove. Ty had not yet finished harassing the pony. And Rowan did not call him again, for Rook stood before her. Rook, whom she had thought was long gone and far from here and maybe even a traitor.

Matter-of-fact as ever, offering her a rag of cloth, he told her, "Your neck is bleeding."

But Rowan barely heard him. She did not lift a hand to accept the cloth, the same bandage she had torn from the hem of her tunic earlier. She could not move for smiling.

"Rook," she told him with all her heart, "thank you. Thank you for going back to find Father."

Flushing red, he ducked his head, turning away from emotion. "Somebody had to have some sense."

"That was what you intended all along, wasn't it?"

"Bah. Bind your neck." He thrust the cloth at her.

Accepting the bandage, Rowan felt her father's hands still resting on her shoulders. "I was going half insane looking for you," Robin said gruffly.

Rook said, "I've never seen a man stride so far so fast, day and night without stopping."

"You did the same," Robin told him.

"I couldn't keep up. You got here first."

Robin seemed not to want to talk about it. "Rowan, let me see that cut."

"It's nothing. A scratch." Rowan turned to hug him again, then sat down beside Celandine's spring to wash her wound.

From under the roots of the great oak, the spring trickled down through flowers and ferns before coming to rest in its stone-lined pool. Wetting her cloth in the stream of water, facing the pool, Rowan saw her own reflected face shining with happiness, radiant like the celandine flowers all around her, blossoms that seemingly shone with their own light in sunset's afterglow.

The face mirrored in the pool was her own, yet not hers alone. Alive in the water, it looked back at her with her mother's eyes.

Rowan felt that look cradle her like an embrace. "Father," she whispered as Robin sat down beside her, "do you see her?"

Apparently not, for he merely took the wet cloth from her hand and started to dab at the blood on her neck.

Rowan blinked, and there was just her own familiar reflection in the pool again. But she knew; she understood. Now she looked into her father's face, noting that he looked very weary and too thin. "Father," she told him tenderly, "I was a fool." *Have they slain her truly?* the aelfe had asked her once, but she had not comprehended until she had seen the glade. "No one killed Mother. She's right here. She always will be. Here, and in me. That is why she had to stay. The only way she might die would be by leaving."

She half expected Robin to give her a worried look and tell her to hush, but he did not. He stilled his hands, studied her face, then nodded. "In her beautiful daughter and in this place," he murmured, glancing around him at celandine flowers like thousands of rayed suns in a green velvet sky. "A place as beautiful as she was. I have never known a lovelier."

"There was reason, after all, for me to venture here. Father." From her ring finger, Rowan slipped off one of the two remaining silver strands of Celandine's ring, and she held it out to him. "I feel as if Mother wants you to have this. As a token that she has not forgotten you."

Robin Hood turned to her, his sky-blue eyes wide.

"And I know for a surety that I want you to have it," Rowan added, "as a token of our love." In this case, Rowan felt certain she could speak for all of the members of the band, but she added, "Especially mine."

She felt a tremor in his fingers as he accepted the

ring from her. She saw his lips move without speaking. She saw his eyes brighten into blue pools of tears.

"Everything's all right, Father. We'll go home now. To Sherwood." Leaning toward him, Rowan placed her healing hands upon his golden head to ease his weariness and give him peace.